To Mary
A Good Friend
& Dedicated
Professional!

Joe L.

To Mari
A Love Friend
& Dedicated
Professional!

Jal.

TRIAL AND COMMITMENT

THE EVENTS LEADING UP TO AND THE
AFTERMATH OF A WEAPONS OF MASS DESTRUCTION EVENT INCLUDING THE
IMPACT ON THE LIVES OF THE PEOPLE WHO EXPERIENCE IT

J. Gasparich

authorHOUSE®

AuthorHouse™
1663 Liberty Drive
Bloomington, IN 47403
www.authorhouse.com
Phone: 1 (800) 839-8640

© 2017 J. Gasparich. All rights reserved.

No part of this book may be reproduced, stored in a retrieval system, or transmitted by any means without the written permission of the author.

Published by AuthorHouse   03/07/2017

ISBN: 978-1-5246-1524-6 (sc)
ISBN: 978-1-5246-1523-9 (e)

Library of Congress Control Number: 2017903077

Print information available on the last page.

Any people depicted in stock imagery provided by Thinkstock are models, and such images are being used for illustrative purposes only.
Certain stock imagery © Thinkstock.

This book is printed on acid-free paper.

Because of the dynamic nature of the Internet, any web addresses or links contained in this book may have changed since publication and may no longer be valid. The views expressed in this work are solely those of the author and do not necessarily reflect the views of the publisher, and the publisher hereby disclaims any responsibility for them.

This book is dedicated to the memory of FDNY BC Orio Joseph Palmer who made the ultimate sacrifice on September 11 in the South Tower of the World Trade Center. Your dedication and sacrifice will never be forgotten!

Chapter 1
A New Career

Michael remembered the accident. He had felt trapped and alone and very cold. The van that he had been a passenger in had hit a patch of ice on Interstate 39 near the Wisconsin and Illinois border as they returned from a weekend getaway in Wisconsin. Michael thought that he might be trapped in the van for a very long time until he caught sight of the firefighter leaving the cab of the fire apparatus. He walked toward Michael and was deliberate in his actions and demeanor. The firefighter spoke kindly to Michael and asked him questions about his life and his trip. The firefighter's professionalism and kindness helped Michael focus on their conversation, and within what seemed like a very few minutes, he was out of the van and on his way to the hospital. Michael never forgot that day or the firefighter's professionalism, and it helped him to pursue a career change at a very key moment in his life.

Michael Fortenier was twenty-two years old. He was a graduate near the top of his class at University of Illinois at Chicago. He was groomed for the medical profession for most of his life so that he could follow closely in his father's footsteps. Michael was a high school athlete, and he had done well for himself at Brother Rice High School and the University of Illinois. Now with the MCAT exam behind him and the college application process done, he had been accepted to the prestigious University of Illinois College of Medicine.

Michael, like many young men, had dreamed of a fire service career. He even visited a firehouse on a high school career day with some of his friends. While it had been a way for the other students to get some free time from school, Michael had left the station with a sense of reverence for the profession. He had become a fan of the Chicago Fire Department and had always had an innate curiosity of what a fire career might hold. He had visited the firehouse near the campus and talked with the firefighters there. They told him that testing was going on in December for a recruit class in January. "You'll have a great career at CFD," they had told him. "It gets in your blood!"

I think it's already in my blood, Michael thought.

So when Michael announced to his family that he was changing professions, he wasn't ready for the reaction that he received. At the dinner table, Michael was shocked to hear his father say, "You're going to do what? Leave the medical profession for the fire service?"

Michael had always admired his father's ability to speak plainly and not mince words. Michael knew that his father's lifelong commitment to his profession had helped him become head of the surgery department at Rush University Medical Center, and he admired his father for that, but he was also hesitant to look his father in the eye. His father continued, "You have been accepted into medical school at University of Chicago. I don't understand."

Michael and his father had talked about the fire career previously, and Michael knew that his father had treated firefighters who had been injured on the job. Michael remembered his father saying to him, "Firefighting is dangerous, and I think many of the people who pursue it as a career have a cavalier attitude toward the profession and to their own health."

Michael's mother was a kind and thoughtful lady who loved her son dearly. She had been his biggest cheerleader throughout his formative years. She was the one person that he trusted above all others in his life. She looked intently at him. "Michael, this is quite a surprise."

This dinner was on the occasion of his mother's fifty-fifth birthday, and the present that he had made for her was a framed picture of them from a recent trip to Hawaii. She placed it on the table next to her and looked at it throughout the evening. Michael was pleased with the gift.

"I tested for the Chicago Fire Department a couple of months ago while I was finishing up my last semester. I didn't think it would happen, but I got in and start the academy next week," Michael answered.

Other than the fire service, Michael's other distraction and passion had been Katy. They had been together for three years, having met in college. Katherine Melinda Menendez was arguably the best-looking woman that he had ever met. Her mother had been a model for the fashion industry when she was younger, and Katy had inherited everything that she had needed to follow in her mother's footsteps. Katy's father had passed away when she was in grade school, and Katy and her mother were everything to each other until Michael appeared in her life. She had accepted him, and so had her mother. Katy was going to be an accountant. She was determined that her looks would always take a backseat to her intellect and determination. She was to start her second semester of her sophomore year in a few days, and Michael was completely infatuated with her. Keeping the fire testing a secret from her was killing him.

Katy looked as though she had just seen a ghost as she looked at Michael over her coffee cup on the opposite side of the table. "You want to be a firefighter? Michael, a firefighter?"

The rest of the meal was one of the most uncomfortable situations Michael had ever been through. He felt like it was the first time that he had ever been in the house that he had spent his teenage years in. There really wasn't much else said about the academy or the fire profession, and when he and Katy left his parents' home, he felt as if he had just told his parents that he had a terminal disease.

They drove in silence in the frigid January temperatures. As Michael walked Katy to the door and turned to give her the familiar good-night kiss, he was hoping that she would ask him to come in. *A glass of wine would be nice*, Michael thought.

"I'm tired, Michael. I'm going to bed." Her words were cold and final.

"I'm sorry that I didn't tell you sooner," Michael told Katy.

"Michael, what the *hell* is wrong with you?" Katy never cursed. "You have it all—a career, a great family, and the chance to make something of yourself. Why throw it all away just to ride a fire truck?"

This was not at all what Michael had expected, planned for, or could ever have imagined.

"Katy, I want to be a firefighter! I want to help people. I want to be part of a great profession. I want to do this, and I want to do this with you by my side."

"This is crazy, Michael." She turned away and unlocked her door. "I'm going to bed. I think this is a bad dream."

Chicago cold is like no other cold. In addition to the frigid temperatures, it is always sharp, and the wind is like a knife that is able to steal all the warmth that the body can generate. For the first time in a very long time, Michael felt that cold.

Michael drove home without the usual chatter of the radio, without the usual warm glow that Katy's presence gave him. He was truly alone.

Chapter 2
Newfound Freedom

Magomed Domechian was a dark-haired, blue-eyed thirty-year-old man. He was born in Chechnya as the son of a well-to-do merchant. He was handsome and articulate and had easily learned English as a second language. He had been through his formative years in school in his home country and had attended Chechen State University. His father's profession never seemed to suit him, and he began buying and selling things on the open market with some friends from school who learned of the narcotics trade in the region. Magomed had been referred to as "Mark" when he began the narcotics business.

When the Russian authorities became aware of his activities, he left and after a few weeks came into the United States on a work visa. He found he was able to make quite a bit of money and fame for himself.

During his time in the narcotics business, Mark had been approached by other sellers to see if he had an interest in the ore business.

Mark had several exchanges with a distributor in his home country. The man only known as Batir had asked Mark if uranium ore was something he wanted to buy and sell.

"I'm happy in my dealings, and I make a lot of money," Mark told Batir.

"You are vulnerable in this business," Batir said to Mark. "You can be more selective in the ore business, and you can move into the shadows when it is best for you to do so."

Batir encouraged Mark to meet his clients, and Mark had done so, but he had established contacts in the narcotics business and the money was far too lucrative.

Mark's days in the narcotics business were numbered. On a cold night in March, the Chicago Police Department and the Cook County Sheriff's Office Drug Task Force raided an apartment where Mark was staying. Mark remembered the raid quite well. He had been awakened from a deep sleep as the door to the apartment was breached by police officers wearing tactical gear. Mark was thrown to the floor, and as he hit the floor, his shoulder had been dislocated. The pain was so intense that Mark almost lost consciousness. The officers confiscated the guns and the money that were in the apartment. Mark was arraigned, and he was quickly tried and was taken to the Illinois Department of Corrections (IDOC) in the Stateville Correctional Center.

After his arraignment, Mark spoke to one of the jailers, who told him, "You were sacrificed by the people you were selling drugs to. You were an easy target."

Mark thought, *How could I have been so stupid? How could I have let this happen to me?*

Mark did not make any friends in prison. He was viewed as an outsider, and those acquaintances that he had were moved to other institutions by the time that Mark had any meaningful companionship with them.

His plan was to go home after he was released from IDOC, but he soon learned through letters from his mother that his father's business was gone. The rebels that had aligned with the radical Muslim factions in the region had demanded that all the businessmen pay a "tax" for security, and his father had declined. His business was gone, and he had not been heard from since. Soon after that, all communications with his family ceased. Mark was very anxious to learn what had happened to his family.

It was also about that same time that a lawyer he was unfamiliar with looked seriously at the court proceedings that had landed Mark in jail. The lawyer known only to him as Mr. Peterson had found inconsistencies in the case, and Mark was released pending a new trial. He was free and back on the streets.

As Mark left the correctional institution, he was met by two men in a dark-colored Chrysler. One of the men looked like a businessman, and the younger man looked like he was something akin to a golf pro or some other type of athletic competitor. Mark had no choice but to approach them. They asked Mark to get into the car with them, and he did so.

The younger man reached over the seat and shook Mark's hand.

"We have heard about you, Mark," the younger man said. "We need your help." This man was obviously a well-spoken gentleman with a bit of a Southern accent. He told Mark his name was Nathan.

"I don't know what you want from me," Mark answered.

Nathan answered, "We want you to talk with your people about something we are trying to acquire. Just ask some questions, that's all, and then we will part company and you can go back and look into your father's affairs."

"Is he alive?" Mark asked quickly.

"We don't know," Nathan said. "Once you help us, we will arrange for you to go back home and see for yourself."

"I don't have any money. The government took everything that I had. They stole it from me!"

Nathan looked directly at Mark and said, "Money is not your problem, my friend. We will get you where you need to go and do it discreetly. You work for us now, and we will get a work permit for you."

"So what do you want? I was in the narcotics business," Mark said.

The vehicle arrived at a business in the city of Chicago, and the men asked Mark to go with them into the business. They entered a well-appointed room with fireplace and furnishings that resembled a boardroom that might be used by a large corporation.

The older man went to a liquor closet and brought out a bottle of imported whiskey that Mark knew must have been worth several hundred dollars. Mark was given a glass. The older man said to Mark, "Enjoy your newfound freedom with some imported whiskey." Mark thanked his host and tasted the whiskey. It was smooth and easy to drink.

Mark enjoyed the first few sips of the whiskey as he felt a tingle pass through his neck and back. This was something that he had not felt in a long time. He relaxed and asked the men, "What is it that you want from me?"

The older man looked at Mark intently. "My name is Simon Waterson, and I want you to work for me. I am in the business of—how shall we say it?—imported and exported goods. I have need of some materials that I believe that you can secure for me."

"Such as?" Mark asked.

"Ore," Nathan stated. "Fissionable uranium ore."

Mark sat the glass down. The liquor was imported, and it was something he was very pleased with. "So you are terrorists, and you want to build a bomb?"

Nathan looked intently at Mark. "We are patriots. We want what is best for our people. The government is corrupt, and the people are suffering. I have hated the government and their imperialistic ideals since I was a young man growing up in the South. I saw my countrymen treated unfairly because of the government's love of segregation and so-called equality. But I must tell you, Mark, that we have another group that we have learned to despise, and that is

Trial and Commitment

the radical fundamentalists. They tried to kill Simon, and for that, they must pay dearly." Nathan's voice rose in pitch and volume as he completed his statement.

Simon raised his hand gently, and Nathan realized that his tone was not becoming of a gentleman. He sat down, and Simon smiled at him and looked at Mark.

"My associate is passionate about our business, as you can see." Simon looked directly at Mark. "Do you trust the government?"

Mark looked at Simon. "Of course not; I hate the government. You know that I do. Almost as much as I hate the radicals or whatever you want to call them. They are fundamentalists that only want death and hardship for the people. They may have killed my family and taken my father's business."

"My friend," Simon stated, "you associated with the wrong kind of losers. They left you exposed to the police, and you were captured and falsely imprisoned. We do not treat our people this way. But I must tell you that we have intentions of dealing a blow to the government and to the radicals as well. To do that, we need uranium ore, but it must be ore that was produced in a foreign country, preferably Ukraine or Russia. That way, it will look like the radicals have carried out the attack, and then the government will finally see to their demise. Then we can continue our business, and we can become the importers and exporters that we want to be."

"Importers?" Mark asked. "What kind of importers?"

Simon looked at Mark and poured another glass of whiskey for him. "Mark, we will tell you more when the time comes, but I must also tell you that one of our associates told us of a man named Batir and a lucrative business that he had established exporting the very ore that we seek."

"Why don't you just deal directly with him yourself?" Mark asked.

"We need an intermediary, so to speak," Nathan answered. "If you do not want to work with us, we understand, but we think you can be of invaluable assistance to us."

Mark looked at the men intently and thought for a few moments. "I was beaten and abused in their so-called correctional institution. I asked for help and received none. I am alone in America, and I hate the government. I will help you, but we must go about this slowly. This is a very intricate process—many shadows and many more snares. No one is who or what they claim to be. I don't even know if Batir is who he claims to be."

Nathan rose from his chair. "You have been through a lot today, my friend. We will take you to an apartment that we have for you, and tomorrow we will show you our business."

With that, the men took Mark to a small but very luxurious apartment that they had for him in South Chicago. The apartment was furnished with fine furniture, and Mark even discovered that the liquor cabinet was filled with a variety of tantalizing liquors. *These people know how to live*, Mark thought. He wasted no time in securing a shower, and he was off to bed before an hour had passed.

Chapter 3
Graduation

Michael and his friend David sat next to each other at graduation from the fire academy. David had been a volunteer firefighter in one of the south suburbs of the city, so he knew a lot of what was being taught.

Michael looked at David. "I want to thank you for helping me through the academy."

"I know that you have a passion for this, and you helped motivate me and the others in the class by your commitment to the training. Besides, who else was going to watch out for you?" David said, and they both laughed.

"I really do appreciate you pushing me through the maze drill, though," Michael said.

The maze drill was something the recruits did several times. The mask of the self-contained breathing apparatus (SCBA) was blackened out with tissue paper, and the recruits had to crawl through tight spaces. They even had to take the SCBA off their backs and crawl through a tight space with the facepiece still in place and then put the air tank and cradle back on their torsos to complete the drill. Michael failed miserably the first time he tried it. The instructors were not impressed with his performance. With David's help, Michael mastered the training evolution after the third try.

The instructors grew to like Michael, as they could see that he was working as hard as he could. They knew he wanted to be a firefighter.

"What did you do before this, Michael?" one of the academy instructors asked him.

Michael let it slip that he had applied to medical school before he could catch himself.

"You were in?" the instructor said.

"Yes. Well, sort of. I hadn't started yet." Michael held his head down.

Michael became known as "Doc" from that day forward in the academy.

The recruit training lasted three months, and Michael was either studying each night or was absolutely exhausted when he got to his apartment. Katy was frustrated both emotionally and physically, as they weren't able to be with each other as much as she wanted.

"I'm trying as hard as I can, babe," Michael told Katy one evening at dinner. As they sat on the couch to watch a movie after dinner, Michael was soon fast asleep.

This was not the life that Katy had hoped for.

After three months, the recruits completed their final evolutions, and graduation day at the Chicago Fire Academy became a reality for the recruits.

Michael was ecstatic!

Graduation day was a big deal for the academy class, and friends and family attended.

Michael's parents and Katy attended. They were there for Michael, but not necessarily because they were happy with Michael's decision.

David's fiancée, Julie, was there as well. She was all smiles.

After the candidates had been announced and the ceremony ended, Michael walked over to his family. His father shook his hand, and his mother hugged him. Katy kissed Michael softly and quickly backed away.

Michael introduced his family to David and Julie.

"David got me through this," Michael told Katy.

Katy smiled sweetly, but it wasn't the best that she could do.

Michael's parents took Katy and Michael to dinner. David and Julie were going to go home to David's apartment, so Michael's father invited them to come along as well.

Michael was pleased that they all got along. Katy and Julie seemed to get along well, and Michael hoped that they could become friends.

The evening ended cordially. Katy and Michael went to his apartment.

"Please try to be accepting of this," Michael said to Katy.

"I'm trying, Michael. It is still sinking in," Katy told him as she turned her head and looked down at the floor.

They watched a movie and drank some wine that Michael had purchased for the evening. Michael was tired, and they called it a night early in the evening. Katy gave him a good-night kiss when he walked her to the door. *Maybe this will be okay,* he thought as he drove home.

Chapter 4
A Nice Place to Work

Chicago Fire Department Station 26 on North Leavitt Street was not exactly where Michael thought that he would begin his tour of duty with CFD, but it was a nice, quiet area with plenty of amenities. With its proximity to the medical district and the interstate, the crews were busy, and the people were good to work with. He had drawn the gold shift with a seasoned crew.

As Michael parked his truck at the station and walked in for his first shift, he was greeted by Captain Charles Smith, who stuck out his hand to Michael and gave him a hug. The first impression that Michael had of Captain Smith was that he looked a lot like Don Cheadle on the television show *House of Lies*.

"Welcome aboard, kid," said Captain Smith, who was a twenty-year veteran of the department. Captain Smith had made his rounds through the city. At forty-two, he decided to settle in at a station with some guys he could work with on the job, and this station seemed to fit his definition of "a nice place to work."

Michael was also greeted by the firefighters on his crew, including Clifton Jones—or Cliff, as he was referred to on the department. Michael took an instant liking to Cliff, as he was a good-natured thirty-year-old firefighter who could have taken Kevin Tighe's place on the show *Emergency*. Cliff had worked in the metals-fabricating industry for five years prior to becoming a firefighter and was glad each day that he got to come to work. "I knew factory life wasn't for me," he told Michael.

Michael also met firefighter Darien James Childers. Darien—or DJ—was thirty-three, and he too had left a profession to become a firefighter. Firefighter Childers had been working as a short-haul truck driver when he too felt the calling to become a firefighter. Michael shook his hand and thought, *He could be a boxer.* DJ was a bookworm and a lover of fitness. He had run the Chicago Marathon the year before and worked hard to be at the peak of physical fitness to complement his job.

Michael was accepted into the station as the men welcomed the opportunity to have a probationary firefighter—or "probie"—and "train him right," as Captain Smith had said. Michael spent the first couple of shifts getting to know the station, the apparatus, and the crew. There was an ambulance housed at the station as well, and Michael was pleased that Cassie McHale was on the ambulance. She had been an instructor at the academy when the crews were given emergency medical services training. Cassie knew about Michael's past, and she knew his father. Cassie was a feisty red-haired lady with fair skin and a smile that could light up a room, but she was also dedicated to the profession and a stern instructor.

"I'm glad that you are here, Michael," Cassie told him when the ambulance came back to the station after a call. "But don't think I'm going easy on you." She laughed and hugged him. Michael laughed as well in a reserved way.

As with most "newbies," there had been some lighter moments, such as the first meal that Michael had prepared. Since the shift was twenty-four hours in length, firefighters normally prepared two meals during the shift. They took turns cooking the meals at the station, and Michael was expected to pull his share of the cooking duties as well. Michael liked to cook, and that was to his advantage. Cliff told Michael, "Go easy on the captain; he likes to eat healthy." Michael decided to really impress the captain, so he prepared a garden salad with grilled chicken and some light pasta on the side. When the crew sat down to dinner with the medics that were at the station, everyone seemed to enjoy the meal except Captain Smith. It was after dinner that Captain Smith looked intently at Michael and said, "Look, kid, I eat healthy at home, I eat healthy when the wife and I go out to dinner, and sometimes I even eat healthy with my kids, but this is the firehouse, and we eat real meat here! Got it?"

"Yes, sir, Captain!" Michael replied.

Cliff and DJ were laughing so hard, they just about fell out of their chairs. "And as far as these two characters are concerned," continued Captain Smith, "they can keep their darned pasta as well!"

The engine crew had its share of emergency medical assist calls and even a couple of working fires thanks to an overheated pot roast and an overstuffed clothes dryer. The firefighters helped Michael along, and somehow the nickname of Doc made its way to the station as well.

When Michael came to work on that Wednesday morning, he had no idea what lay in store for him. Michael had stopped by Katy's apartment before work for coffee. "I think this will be a good day," Michael said to Katy.

"I hope it is an uneventful day so that my stomach isn't tied in knots all day," Katy said.

"It's okay, Katy. I work with a good crew that wants me to do well, and they take care of me."

"Michael, you don't understand. I don't care how great they are, and I believe you, but you go into situations that are bad when you get there, and they sometimes get worse."

"Katy, I love you, and I will be all right," Michael said.

They parted ways. *This is a roller coaster*, Michael thought. He was also concerned that he had seen some papers from the University of Missouri–St. Louis on the counter, but he didn't think much more of it

When he got to work, Cliff had a cup of coffee ready for him. *I really like this guy*, Michael thought.

They enjoyed their coffee and began the daily checks of the apparatus.

"How's the bride-to-be?" asked Cliff as he helped Michael check the air in the bottles in each air pack.

Michael just shrugged.

"That good, huh?" replied Cliff.

Michael told Cliff, "*Bride* is definitely not something she has on her mind right now."

Michael and Cliff began inspecting the SCBAs on the engine. There were four SCBAs and two spares in the rear compartment of the engine. The compartment also contained four spare air bottles that could be secured in the air packs when the first bottles had low air pressure.

The SCBAs on the engine were the firefighters' lifelines. The bottles contained air that was fit for breathing when the firefighters entered an atmosphere that was full of smoke or an atmosphere where the concentration of oxygen in the air was less than 19 percent.

Proper use of SCBA was taught from almost the first day of the academy. You learned how to put them on (donning), how to take them off (doffing), and how to turn on the air bottles and check the air pressure constantly. The SCBAs became part of the trainees' bodies when they had them on.

Michael remembered the training that he had been through in the academy with the SCBA. The instructors had told Michael, "This is twenty-five pounds of aluminum, rubber, and fiberglass composite, but before you are done with this training, it will feel like part of your body." Michael had to admit that before the academy was over, he had learned to walk while wearing the SCBA, crawl while wearing the SCBA, and even sit while wearing the SCBA. But there wasn't much sitting when you had it on.

They closed the doors, and Michael told DJ, "I think pack two has a leak; the bottle's down about a third from yesterday."

"The other crew filled it last night," DJ said.

"Better get it checked out. I'll pull it off and change it out once the rest of the inspection is done," Cliff stated. He looked at Michael. "What's up with Katy? Doesn't she know this is what you want to do? And firefighters can beat up on doctors any day!" They all laughed. "By the way, where's the ambulance?"

Captain Smith walked in as he asked the question. "They are on the Eisenhower Expressway on an EMS Plan 1. I'm surprised we didn't get that one, but hey, I guess they are keeping us for something else."

The Chicago Fire Department had their own sets of dispatching codes. An EMS Plan 1 was used to inform dispatchers and the response organization how many ambulances would be dispatched. If engines or trucks were dispatched along with the ambulance, and a supervisor. A box card is a prewritten set of instructions for dispatchers and responders that delineates what personnel and equipment would be dispatched to each call. The Chicago Fire Department's box cards covered a very wide range of emergency situations.

DJ begin to tell the chief that he thought they might need to switch the second air pack out when that something that was waiting just for them came to pass!

The radio signal broke the conversation that the men were having. "Engine 26, respond to a report of smoke in a building near the 1400 block of West Flournoy. Caller states smoke showing.

Trial and Commitment

Time out: 0845." The dispatcher was calm and methodical in her announcement.

A Chicago fire engine is a well-tuned machine of people and equipment. Each person knows his or her job and how that will be accomplished without much communication. Even in his short time on the department, Michael had been taught by the men on his crew what was to be done. His main job was to don his SCBA and get the irons, which consisted of a pick-head ax and a Halligan bar to help make entry into a structure. He would then help search and clear the structure or help with extinguishment by backing up the firefighter who was manning the hose line. It was hot, hard, dirty, and rewarding work, and it was all accomplished as a team.

Michael grabbed his gear and slipped into his bunker pants. As he was grabbing his coat and helmet, the Detroit diesel engine that powered Engine 26 roared to life. The firefighters kept their gear on the floor of the bay near the engine at all times so that they could get dressed quickly. As Michael was zipping his coat after he climbed into his seat, the engine left the station and headed south.

DJ was seated directly in front of Michael, as he was driving. Cliff was seated next to Michael, and Captain Smith was in the right seat, or command position. It was his engine; he called the shots.

"Control from 26, any info on occupancy?" Captain Smith asked as he picked up the microphone from the hanger on the doghouse, or engine cover, that covered the engine that powered the vehicle.

"Twenty-six from Control, it was a cell phone call into 411 that was routed to us; no other info available. Sorry."

411 is the city's information number, not the preferred method to report an emergency. Two call takers had already handled the caller. Much information may have already been lost.

"Well, men, this is what we trained for, so let's suck it up!" Captain Smith laughed and smiled at Michael. "This what it's all about, kid."

"Geez, Captain, I feel like we're in the movie *Armageddon*," stated Michael.

"I love that movie," Cliff said.

"Twenty-six from Control. Better address: 1407 West Flournoy."

"Message received, Control, and 26 will be arriving on scene. Heavy smoke showing," Captain Smith said as he conducted a windshield size-up of the incident.

Along with Engine 26 was another engine that was already en route. Also dispatched were two trucks that were fire apparatus without pumps but equipped with ladders. The firefighters on the truck were there to help with entry into the building and to help ventilate, or open up, the structure if necessary, even to the point of cutting the roof. There were command personnel en route as well and ambulances.

Trial and Commitment

"We have a three-story brick structure with smoke on the first floor, possibly extending to the second story," Captain Smith told the dispatcher.

Michael was off the engine and putting on the air pack. *Just like the academy*, he thought. *Slow and steady wins the race.* Michael was securing the chest straps, adjusting the waist strap, and checking the mask for a seal before he tightened it down. He thought, *Now pull the hood over the mask and get the helmet on.*

"Doc, let's go!" Cliff yelled. "Get the irons!"

"Irons, gloves, helmet … c'mon," Michael muttered to himself as he opened the back compartment of the engine. He grabbed the irons and ran to Cliff.

Engine 107 was just arriving on the scene, but since DJ had secured his pump on the engine and had a charged hose line, the engines crew would take the hose line in that DJ had secured. They had also to charge a line, but that would be for the backup team once they had geared up.

DJ took pump operations very seriously. He had taken classes on pump operations at the academy, and he knew pump pressures, water flow, and pump mechanics as well as anyone in the department. He had water in the hose within a minute.

Michael and Cliff headed to the door to begin a search of the first floor.

"Stay with me, kid!" Cliff looked Michael in the eyes. "You can do this. Slow your breathing down, and let's get it done!"

Michael had been a believer in physical fitness since high school, and he had continued to run and lift weights. It had paid off in the academy. Michael hoped it would pay off today. He concentrated on his breathing and tried to take deeper breaths.

As Cliff and Michael got to the door, they tried it, and it was unlocked and swung freely. Cliff pushed it open, and he and Michael began to crawl in to begin a primary search. Their job was to check each room methodically and then to do the same on the second and third floors. Following closely behind them was the attack crew whose only job was to find the seat of the fire and extinguish it.

As they went into the first room, they managed to make their way around the furniture in the front room and move quickly through. By using the irons, they were able to extend their reach to get to the walls of the room.

"This room's clear!" Cliff yelled through the facepiece. "Let's get to the next room on the right on the first floor!"

As Michael and Cliff moved from the front room, the attack crew passed by them toward the kitchen, where the fire appeared to be.

They found a door that led to a bedroom. Michael was aware that it was getting hotter as they went in. He saw what appeared to be light from a partially opened window. Something told him that there had been a lecture in academy that said, "If you're going to find them, look by the windows!" He began to feel around the room. *What in the world is that?* he thought. *A foot?*

Michael Fortenier was experiencing something that a firefighter fears, dreads, and hopes for all in one breath. It was not the cold, hard foot of a mannequin that they used at the academy. It was a real human foot!

"Cliff, I got a body!" Michael screamed into the mask.

His friend was literally on top of him before the words got out. It was hard to hear each other with the SCBA facepieces on, but Michael got the words out without any hesitation.

"Grab the legs!" Cliff yelled. "Let's get 'em out now!"

Michael didn't remember much about the trip out except that he heard his air pack low-air alarm almost as soon as he shouted to Cliff. They managed to get the patient out the door and into the front walk in front of the structure. It was then that Michael realized that he had just carried a woman out of a burning house.

An ambulance crew was running toward them. Michael recognized that the paramedic was Cassie. "Is she breathing, Michael?" she asked.

"No. Well, maybe. I'm not sure. She needs suction!" Michael said. Cliff was checking for a pulse as Cassie and her partner, a young man who didn't look much older than Michael, began to use a portable suction unit to clear the lady's upper airway. What was coming from the lady's mouth was a combination of carbon, saliva, and mucous. Michael fought back the desire to vomit as he felt himself start to sweat and his throat get dry.

Cliff and Cassie were working to get the patient ready for the defibrillator. With a quick slit like the hands of a surgeon, Cliff had the lady's T-shirt removed, and he and Cassie attached the leads.

"She's in v-fib!" Cassie said to Michael and Cliff. Ventricular fibrillation is a heart rhythm that is unproductive. The heart was not beating rhythmically and was not functioning properly.

Michael looked at the monitor. His clinical time in the last year of college told him what he was seeing: this heart rate was nonproductive; no blood flow, just random electrical activity. Michael moved from the head to start chest compressions.

"Get the IV in," Cassie instructed.

Cassie and Cliff were working frantically. Cliff was trying to get the veins on the back of the lady's hand to appear so that he could insert the catheter.

"No veins," he replied.

"Put the tourniquet on closer to the hand," Michael told him.

Cliff looked at him and moved the tourniquet down the arm. The veins began to become more noticeable.

"Okay, I'm in!" Cliff told Cassie as he got the IV established and the fluids began to flow. Cassie was working with the monitor to evaluate the heart rhythm.

"Push the epi," Cassie said. "Push it now before we lose what we have."

Epinephrine is a drug that has been referred to as a wonder drug by many who work in the EMS field. It is a pharmaceutical form of adrenaline. Adrenaline is produced by the body in times of crisis or stress to increase the performance of the bodily functions.

"C'mon, c'mon, lady," Cassie murmured.

Cliff was pushing the drug in through the intravenous line by using a syringe.

Cassie's cool blue eyes were as big as saucers. Michael had never seen her like this. She was always so methodical when she taught them at the academy. She was always in control. Michael was in awe of her intensity.

"There! There! Coarse v-fib! See it, Michael?" Cassie said in a high-pitched voice. "Get ready to shock her!"

The monitor charged to the predetermined amperage, and a green light came on.

"Clear, Michael. Get away from her, or we'll have two to work on!"

"Yes, clear." Michael backed away.

The shock was not at all like what was seen in the movies, and the paddles were pads attached to the chest with a sticky film. The shock did not even cause the patient to jump. But the amperage did its job. The defibrillator actually stopped the heart so that the normal conduction system of the heart would again pick up the inherent heart rhythm—and if it did, blood would begin to flow through the heart again.

As Michael stared at the monitor, all he saw was a flat line, but then suddenly, the familiar heart rate rhythm began to emerge.

"Wow," Michael stated.

"Bag her, bag her. Get her some oxygen," Cassie told Cliff.

Cliff began to squeeze the plastic ambu bag.

"Let's load her! We gotta go!" Cassie told the firefighters. Captain Smith had brought the stretcher over from the ambulance. They loaded the lady onto the stretcher and took her to the ambulance. Michael helped load the patient. Cliff climbed in the ambulance to assist the paramedics on the way to the hospital a few short blocks away.

Once the door on the ambulance was shut, Michael became aware that he had on no SCBA, no coat, and no helmet. *Where did I lose all that?* he thought.

He walked over to Captain Smith.

"Get some water, and now I know why they call you *Doc*. 'Move the tourniquet, Cliff.'" Captain Smith slapped him on the back. "Good job, junior."

As Captain Smith laughed and walked away to talk with the other officers, Michael looked up.

She had been standing there all along, and their eyes met. Michael instantly recognized her. She was taller than he imagined, and her eyes were as dark as night. Her fair skin almost looked out of place for her features, but she was more beautiful than he could have imagined.

"I'm Marie, from Channel 2," she said to Michael. "May I talk to you about what just happened?"

"Uh, sure. I mean, I can't. Sorry," Michael sputtered. *She has beautiful eyes*, he thought. "I know who you are. I've seen you on the late news," Michael said.

"Are you a new firefighter?" she asked.

"Yes, I am, but you have to talk to the captain," Michael told her. "That's protocol."

"The captain wasn't working on the patient, and he didn't pull her out of the building. Yes, I saw it. We were on our way to Rush when we got the call," Marie told Michael.

Marie McCleary was a staple on the Channel 2 late news at 10:00. She had broken into the Chicago news scene two years before after a brief stint at a television news station in Nashville. She was determined, intelligent, and beautiful, and that combination had helped Channel 2 get the ratings for the 10:00 p.m. spot. At twenty-five, she was an industry standard.

Captain Smith walked over to Marie and Michael. "Okay, ma'am, no manhandling the probies," Captain Smith told Marie. "Our public information officer is on the way, and we are at a loss stopped."

Loss stopped meant that operations were wrapping up. The fire was out, and the hoses were being drained and reloaded onto the engines. The ladders were coming down, and the firefighters were preparing to leave the scene.

"The fire investigator will look that scene over, but my guess was food on the stove, and that's all you get, Ms. Marie," Captain Smith stated.

Michael got up off the tailboard of the engine and walked toward Marie. "It was nice to meet you," he said.

"Likewise, Mr. Probie." Marie looked at him. "Do you have a name?"

"Michael—my name is Michael." He gave a halfhearted smile. "I hope that the lady makes it."

"You gave her a chance, Michael," Marie told him.

As Michael walked toward the engine, Marie continued to watch him.

"Marie. Earth to Ms. Marie. I shot some video," her cameraman stated. "Can we please go to Rush and get the interview done now?"

"Uh, sure, sure," Marie said. She watched Michael and the others get into the engine.

Chapter 5
A Legitimate Business

Mark met with Nathan and Simon at their warehouse on Chicago's South Side.

"This is our business. You will help us here," Nathan told Mark.

The business was a wholesale food warehouse on the South Side of Chicago.

"We import and distribute fine wine, cheese, and pasta throughout the Midwest," Nathan told Mark. "The business has been here many years and is very legitimate."

They walked back to a small office where Simon was working on the computer. There were at least one dozen workers loading and unloading trucks in the building, which had obviously been something other than a warehouse at some point in its history.

Mark looked at Simon. "So I will be working for you here?"

"Yes," Simon replied. "This will be your place of employment. Mark, it is imperative that we act quickly to get the material purchased and shipped to us here."

"I'm not sure if I can make contact with these people in such a short period of time. I will have to reestablish some contacts."

"How much time do you need?" Nathan asked.

"A week, two weeks, maybe more."

Simon looked at Nathan, and he seemed perplexed.

"Nathan," Mark continued. "This isn't like walking into a supermarket in Chicago and saying, 'Please give me some fissionable uranium, Russian or Ukrainian variety, please.' You have to establish contacts, work the system, be sure that who you are talking to is who you are really talking to. I don't even know if the people that I dealt with are still around—or alive, for that matter—and if they can even tell me who I need to talk to."

Simon spoke up. "Okay, okay, we see what you are saying."

Mark continued, "If I can find it. How do I—or *we*—get it here? You can't walk around in the southern part of Russia with a radioactive package. Russian troops shoot first and ask questions later, especially in the area where I will be going. The Chechen rebels aren't exactly friends with the Russian Federation, and the radical groups aren't exactly playing the game there either."

Nathan looked at Mark. "You are the buyer. We will get it here."

Simon looked at Mark. "Report here for work each day. You can work in the warehouse, and when the trucks are gone, we will give you an office to work from. Go and buy what you need. We buy TracFones and wireless devices all over the city, and then they end up in Lake Michigan after we use them. We will have secure Internet unless we need to remote that from cards as well."

"Could you secure transportation for me as well?" Mark asked Simon.

"We have a car dealer that we work with, and they export used cars," Simon said. "We can get you something cheap to drive."

"What if I want a BMW or Mercedes?" Mark asked. "Can you get me one of those?"

"We can get you something cheap to drive," Nathan replied. "Let's go and see what we can get for you."

The two walked out the door and left the building.

Chapter 6
A Relationship That Ends

"I hope that we can have a great evening," Michael said to Katy. "You look really nice tonight!"

Michael had taken Katy to her favorite restaurant in the city for dinner. Michael and Katy liked this nice Greek restaurant. It was clean, quiet, and had a very nice atmosphere. The smell of lamb, chicken, and other meats being prepared was all around them, as was the occasional "Opa!" as the flaming cheese was cooked to perfection and then sprinkled with a light lemon sauce.

The waiter stopped at the table. "Something to drink, my friends?"

"Water, please," said Katy.

"Something on draft?" Michael asked.

As the waiter highlighted items on the list, Michael noticed that Katy was looking at the table.

"A light beer is fine," he told the waiter.

"Be right back with the drinks," the waiter said.

"Michael, I want to tell you something," Katy began.

Michael looked up from the menu directly into her eyes, and she looked down again. *What is going on here?* he thought.

"When you went into the fire service, I wasn't happy, but I thought, all right, let's give it a try." Katy paused and took his hand. "When we went to dinner and drinks with your station crew the other day, I'll be honest, I was jealous because they have your heart right now."

"Katy, you have my heart," Michael told her.

"Please, Michael, please let me finish. When we first met, all I wanted was for you to say that you loved me, and when you did, I thought my world would be complete, and all I ever feared was losing you to someone else."

The waiter arrived with the drinks. "Here you go," he said. "Would you like to order an appetizer?"

"Thanks," Michael said. "Maybe in a minute."

"Of course, sir." The waiter walked toward the kitchen.

Michael said, "Katy, if you are telling me that this is over, I can't believe it. I won't believe it!"

"Michael, I haven't lost you to anyone," Katy said. "I've lost you to something that you love more than me, and I can't compete with this career."

"Katy, I love you because you make me complete," Michael said. "I can't believe that we won't make this work. I can balance the job and our relationship. I know I can."

"Michael, I was at work the other day when you had the fire, and I think what you did was amazing. We were watching the noon news, and the newspeople said something about a fire and someone trapped, and all I could say to myself was …" She paused and took a deep breath. "'Please don't let it be him.' I saw you there on the television." Katy was tearing up. "I can't bear the thought of—"

The waiter returned. "May I get you something?"

Michael was getting up from the table. "I'm sorry, but could we please have the check? I think we will be leaving."

The waiter said, "You have been here many times; please just be careful and come again. I will take care of it."

"Thanks," Michael said, and he put a twenty-dollar bill on the table.

"She is a nice lady, sir. Have a good night," the waiter said as he walked away.

Michael helped Katy put on her coat, and they walked to the car.

When they arrived at Katy's house, Michael said, "You don't have to say it, but maybe we can let things calm down a bit and see what else happened between us."

"I accepted an offer for an internship in St. Louis." Katy began to cry. "I think it will give me the chance to think through some things and get my priorities straightened out."

Michael didn't say anything. He leaned over and kissed her on the forehead. "I'm sorry."

"It's not your fault, Michael, and I've never seen you this happy. You hated premed in college; I knew it, and so did you," Katy went on. "Studying for the MCAT exam was hell for you. I knew you'd end up doing something else. You only did it because your dad wanted you to. I just never thought you'd end up here. I just can't be a firefighter's wife. I'm sorry."

The drive home was surreal. It was like part of his life had just died. Michael was in emotional pain. His life was being torn apart at the core, and the feeling was something that resonated from his head right through his core. Katy, the girl he wanted to marry, was leaving. Michael had always tried to think rationally, but this defied any rationality. His head was spinning, and he couldn't believe what had happened.

Michael unlocked his front door, opened it, stepped inside, and sank to the floor with his head in his hands. He began to cry. "Katy ..."

Chapter 7
Lazarus

Michael was sitting with Cliff and DJ after lunch.

It had been a busy morning with two EMS assists and a clothes dryer overheating in a Laundromat near the fire station.

"You know, Michael," Cliff said, "people change, and Katy changed based on how you changed." He was commenting on what Michael had told them about Katy. "We've all been through these things—maybe not to the level that you have, but we have all been there."

Michael restated what Cliff had said. "She changed because I changed, and then she changed—that's confusing even to me."

DJ said, "It's a bad deal, Doc, but just give it and her time and see what comes of it."

"I know, guys, and I appreciate what you are trying to do, but I have to deal with this in my own way," Michael said.

Trial and Commitment

"Yeah, but just keep talking," Cliff said. "Don't clam up, 'cause then all I have to listen to is these other two, and they confuse me."

"I heard that!" Captain Smith said from his office as he worked on the morning's paperwork.

The doorbell rang, and Captain Smith went to answer it, as he was standing in the hallway by then.

"Yes, they are here," he said. "Certainly. Come in, please."

Captain Smith walked through the door into the dayroom, escorting a lady and a young man. The lady appeared to be in her early forties, and she had long dark hair and deep blue eyes. She was obviously in great physical shape for her age, and she carried herself well. She was holding a box of chocolates and a card.

"My name is Amy, and I wanted you to have these. We kinda know each other already, but I don't know if you remember me. We unofficially met last Tuesday on Flournoy Street," she said with a smile.

Michael's jaw dropped open. "Yes, ma'am, we did!"

Cliff suddenly realized who the lady was, as he had ridden with her to the hospital in the ambulance. He, too, was without words.

"Please, ma'am, sit down—and you too, sir," Captain Smith stated. "May I get you something to drink?"

"No, sir," Amy stated. "Thank you. This is Dan, my fiancé."

Dan shook the firefighters' hands and sat down. "I'm pleased to meet you gentlemen. I don't get to shake the hands of heroes all that often. Well, actually never." He smiled at them.

Amy began, "I am a nurse on the respiratory floor at Rush, and Dan and I are going to be married in a few months, so I have been working extra hours to prepare for the wedding and honeymoon. The other day, the day of the fire, I put some meat in the oven to sear before I put it in the Crock-Pot to simmer all day so that we could have a nice dinner. I guess I dozed off, and the next thing I know, I wake up in ICU."

Dan said, "You can't imagine how I felt when I got the call that she was in ER and that there had been a fire. But when I got there, they were already moving her to intensive care, and her breathing and heart rate were really good. It was a miracle—well, actually, there were two miracles, and I guess we are looking at them."

Cliff spoke up. "We're just firefighters, that's all we are and do. We are glad that you are alive and doing really well. Right, Doc? I mean, *Michael*?"

Michael was still in awe, but he managed to get out, "Yep, right, Cliff. Right." *She has the bluest eyes*, he thought, *and I never even saw them when I was with her.*

Amy said, "There was no pain, really, and I felt like I was floating. Then I woke up intubated, and they had to increase the Valium they were giving me." She laughed. "I don't remember anything about the whole event other than waking up in the ER, but as soon as I woke up in the room, I just knew that everything would be all right, and I felt like someone had cared for me that knew exactly what to do to help me."

They talked for the next few minutes about the wedding and what she and Dan were going to do after the wedding. Amy wanted to know about Michael and Cliff and the rest of the station crew and the medics. When they got to Cassie, Amy smiled and said, "I know her; I think everyone at the hospital does."

"Is there anything that you need from us?" Captain Smith asked. "We would be glad to help out any way that we can."

Amy looked at Cliff and Michael and said, "You have already done everything for me. You helped me to get my life back. I can't ask for any more."

Amy and Dan got up to leave. She looked at Michael and Cliff. "I'm glad you are both firefighters. I'm really glad to be alive. I have so much to live for! But before I go, I want one thing if it is allowed. I want a hug from each of you."

"Oh yes, ma'am," Captain Smith stated. "Hugging is definitely allowed here." He laughed out loud.

Amy hugged Cliff, and then she turned to Michael. "You are going to be a great firefighter!"

She gave Michael a long hug and held on. Michael began to tear up. *Stop it*, he thought. She kissed him on the cheek. "Thanks again."

The firefighters showed their guests to the door and talked a bit on the drive before Amy and Dan got in Dan's car and left. As they pulled out of the drive, the men didn't say anything to each other. Captain Smith finally spoke up as he cleared his throat. "You boys make me proud. There isn't a better crew in the city."

Michael spent a lot of quiet time for the rest of that shift sitting on the tailboard of the engine looking out into the sky. *Maybe I am doing something right!*

Chapter 8
Logistics of Travel

Mark sat down in the chair near Simon's desk.

"Did we get you something to drive?" Simon asked.

Mark replied, "Yes, a beautiful blue Chevrolet Impala police pursuit vehicle."

"I'm sure it will serve your needs," Simon replied.

Mark shrugged. "A beautiful blue BMW would have been better."

"Patience, my friend, patience," said Simon.

Simon was dialing his telephone on his desk.

"Hello," a voice on the phone broke in.

"Yes, Mr. Peterson," Simon spoke up. "This is Simon Waterson."

"Yes, Simon, what can I do for you?" Mr. Peterson said.

"Mr. Peterson, we need to secure a passport for our friend Magomed to travel overseas. Can you get one for us, please?" Simon asked.

There was a long pause. "Simon, I knew after reviewing his case that we could get him out of jail because of inconsistencies in the prosecution's evidentiary trail, but this is a whole different matter. Even though I got the charges dropped, Magomed is going to be on the no-fly list and maybe even the terrorism watch list. This is not a matter of evidence but of government oversight."

Simon replied, "We can pay for this."

Mr. Peterson replied, "Simon, I do not deny that. You have been very fair with me, but this will be very difficult to do. What would be the reason, may I ask?"

Simon replied, "He has an ailing father in Chechnya that he would like to visit."

After another long pause, Mr. Peterson said, "I will see the judge today, and then I will meet with the Homeland Security officials in Chicago and see if I can secure a passport. The judge is, I think, the key to getting this done. He has some friends who he can work with in Homeland Security. As you know, he has a strong affinity for imported Irish whiskey, and he likes the baseball tickets."

Simon answered, "They will be forthcoming today."

Trial and Commitment

Mr. Peterson said, "He will only have a few days on the passport before he will have to return to the States."

"I understand," said Simon. "Thank you." He hung up the phone.

Simon turned to Mark. "How long will it take for you to meet with these people?"

"Not long. I will have to change the meeting location," Mark replied. "I do not even know if my father is alive."

Simon stated, "I can assure you he is. We have some friends in the Red Crescent who have located him. We sent him some money and provisions through them. They were willing to help after we assured them a sizeable donation."

Mark asked, "Why are you doing this for me?"

"You have valuable skills, and you know how to negotiate," Simon replied.

"I'm a two-bit criminal that has spent my life running from the law and myself," Mark answered.

"Magomed," answered Simon, "when we get what we need after you have helped us secure it, you can go where you please with enough money to make you happy. You can go and get your father and go to Argentina, Africa, Australia, anywhere you want to go. So, you see, your life is not a failure."

Mark sat there and contemplated his situation. "I hope I can get what you need."

"I'm sure you will get the materials for us," Simon replied. "Now you do need to know that we will route all the transactions through a bank in Greece. Their banking system is in some confusion, shall we say, and nothing can be tracked through there."

"I understand," Mark replied. "I will go and load some cheese on trucks."

"All part of a day's work," replied Simon.

Chapter 9
A Meeting in Time

Michael and Cliff decided that they should indulge in meal that was absolutely delicious but did not meet Cliff's definition of a "salad lunch." They picked a restaurant on Taylor Street that specialized in roast beef and all the trimmings, including fries and milk shakes.

"This might be the closest thing to heaven on earth," Cliff said as they pulled up to the restaurant.

As they parked the department pickup truck and walked to the restaurant, Michael caught sight of a man eating his lunch on a picnic table near the entrance. They exchanged glances, and Michael thought no more of it.

Michael and Cliff ordered their lunches and were walking out of the restaurant when the man spoke to Michael. "I see that you are a firefighter."

The gentleman was Mark.

"Yes, I am, sir," Michael replied.

"I saw you on television the other day," Mark said. "You helped rescue a woman who was in a fire."

Michael was surprised that the man remembered his face the story that Marie had done on the fire. This was Chicago, and random exchanges on the street weren't very common. The man's accent intrigued Michael, and he moved toward the man to engage in a short conversation.

"Yes, it was me," Michael said quietly.

"My name is Mark. I think you did a great thing. You are dedicated to helping people."

They shook hands.

"I'm a firefighter," Michael said. "That's what we do. There is good in everyone that you meet. We just try to help people out."

Mark looked intently at Michael. "Well, you did a great job."

Michael smiled, and he and Cliff walked toward the truck. Cliff went around the truck and opened the door for Michael. "Let me get that for you, oh great one," Cliff said and chuckled.

"Clifton Jones, you are a smarty-pants," Michael said and laughed.

"Good thing I'm really your hero so you don't take yourself too seriously," Cliff said.

They both smiled.

Michael shook his head. "And you are modest too."

They drove away.

Mark watched the firefighters get in the truck and leave. *They are friends as well*, he thought.

Mark thought about the exchange with Michael the rest of the day.

Chapter 10
A New Opportunity

"Media day ... great," said Cliff. "How did we draw this highly coveted duty?"

Captain Smith answered, "You know as well as I do that some engine gets pulled out of service for this each year, and this year it was our turn, I guess."

Media day is a day at the Chicago Fire Academy when the local media stations send their reporters to "play firefighter." They wear turnout gear and SCBAs if they want to. They crawl in tight places, pull mannequins, handle charged handlines, and even go into a smoke-filled room. They get to see what the life of a firefighter is truly like.

DJ said, "I still think it is because of the media star in the back." He pointed at Michael.

Michael shook his head. "I'm the probie, remember, Mr. DJ?"

DJ and Cliff laughed.

Cliff said, "Well, at least he opened up a bit!"

Michael had kept to himself, and he wasn't sleeping well. Katy was gone. Her possessions were gone from his apartment with a note on the table with the key. The note said, "I hope that things go well for you. I will always cherish our relationship, and yes, Michael, I have always loved you!" The words were like a knife each time he read them. Michael felt like his heart was torn open.

"Hey, hotshot. Maybe Ms. Marie will be there," Cliff said.

Michael looked up quickly. "Marie! Oh, the lady from Channel 2!"

"The one who watched you from the time she got on scene till we rolled after the fire," DJ said. "Yep, I watched her keeping an eye on you."

Michael began to blush. "She is beautiful."

"We finally got a live one here," DJ told Captain Smith.

Captain Smith just shook his head and rolled his eyes. "Kids," he muttered.

They pulled in front of the academy. "Meeting in the main classroom, boys," Captain Smith said. "Let's go."

Marie and her camera operator pulled up in front of the fire academy. "Let's park on the ramp across the street," Marie told Freddy.

"We aren't assigned to media day, Marie." Freddy Kunkle had been Marie's cameraman since her first day on the job in Chicago news. "They are sending the new kid that handles the city beat." Freddy said.

"I just want to stop by for a little while, and then we can head downtown," Marie added.

"Okay, but you're the one who gets the butt-chewing if we are late," Freddy replied.

The news reporters were assigned to stations at the academy for the day's training session, and they rotated through each station. The toughest and most important station was the pepper smoke in the training cans. Michael and Captain Smith agreed to work that station, and David was there too. Michael had not seen David since graduation. Michael was glad to see him again.

"I heard about Katy," David said. "I'm sorry, man."

"It's tough," Michael replied. "I guess it was going to happen sooner or later."

"How's your dad handling all this?" David asked.

"He doesn't say much," Michael replied. "I think he thinks it's just a phase I'm going through."

"Some phase," replied David. "Like pulling a lady out of a burning house. Those things just come and go." They both laughed.

Marie and Freddy made their way onto the training grounds.

The battalion chief asked them, "Credentials? Are you registered for this, Ms. Marie?"

"I, uh, forgot to bring them," Marie replied. "You can call the newsroom if you'd like."

"Go ahead," replied the battalion chief. "You pretty much go wherever you want to anyway."

"But I always make you guys and gals look good!" Marie replied.

"Well, that you do. All right, you can go and see the show," the battalion chief replied. "Just be careful on the carnival rides."

"Marie, we are gonna get dinged for this," Freddy said.

Marie didn't hear him, or at least she acted like she didn't.

Michael was helping a young reporter from a major news Chicago affiliate get the SCBA on his back.

"It sure is heavy," the young man stated.

If the tank didn't weigh as much as you did, Michael thought.

"What about my glasses? Can I wear my glasses? How do you firefighters wear all this? Isn't it hot?" the young man continued.

"No, and—" Michael stopped in midsentence. Marie was looking intently at him.

"No glasses," Captain Smith said. "Here, let me help you. My main man here just had a transient ischemic attack of the brain!" He took the mask out of Michael's hands. "Oh brother," he said.

"What are you doing here?" Michael asked. "You surely have been here before."

"You wouldn't believe how many times," Freddy muttered.

Marie gave him a look that indicated that he should probably not say any more.

"There isn't any documented footage of me in the full turnout gear," Marie stated. "I want some—footage, that is." Her face got red.

Captain Smith and David got the young reporter dressed in the turnout gear, and the young man had had all he wanted of it, so he doffed his gear and handed it to Michael. "Fix her up," Captain Smith told him, and he and David went over to the tailboard of the engine and sat down.

Marie looked at Michael. "You heard the man."

"Yes, ma'am," replied Michael. "Take off the watch and the earrings. You know the game." Michael could not stop looking at Marie. She was beautiful, and for one brief instant, the pain of Katy's absence was gone. *What's going on here?* Michael thought. He realized he was staring at Marie and that she was one of the most beautiful women that he had ever seen. He was staring intently at her necklace. His face got red. "The necklace . . . uh, the necklace should be taken off too." Michael was stuttering.

Marie removed the items and handed them to Freddy, who was setting up the tripod to set the camera on and film it all. Michael was somewhat jealous that she had not handed the items to him. He glared at Freddy.

Michael sat Marie down on the chair and helped her take off her shoes. They carefully placed her feet in the fire boots, and Michael helped her up and lifted and buckled the bunker pants. He then helped Marie place the suspenders over her shoulders. *She has strong shoulders*, Michael thought.

"Okay, here's the coat," Michael said. Marie put the coat on, and Michael showed her how to zip it up and shackle it. He took the helmet and helped her get it on her head, and they adjusted it.

"Okay, Marie," Michael said. "You look like a real firefighter." David handed him the air pack.

"Do you want to wear this?" Michael asked.

"Do firefighters wear it?" asked Marie. She obviously knew the answer.

As they placed the SCBA on her back, Michael and Marie had a bit of a problem getting it over her shoulders.

"Maybe you should loosen the chest straps?" Captain Smith said. He could barely get the words out.

He and David both stepped around the engine to keep from laughing out loud.

"Oh, sure," Michael said. He suddenly realized that Marie was staring right into his eyes. His face got red again.

But soon Marie was all set up and ready to go. As Michael turned on the SCBA, it buzzed, and the diaphragm in the mask seated and popped softly.

"Now just let me put this over your face, and when I get it there, take a deep breath and you will be on the air in the SCBA," Michael told Marie.

"All right, Michael," Marie said. The game was just about up: Marie was claustrophobic. She allowed Michael to place the mask over her face. Her dark eyes were totally dilated. But she took a deep breath, and something magical happened. She was breathing from the mask, and she wasn't scared at all. Freddy had anticipated the impending meltdown and was ready with the camera rolling.

Michael took Marie by the hand and walked her around the training grounds. He wasn't aware that most of the rest of the stations had stopped what they were doing to observe the Chicago Fire Academy's version of *Dancing with the Stars*.

As Michael helped Marie get the mask and gear off, he looked at her. They were alone. Freddy had wandered off to talk with a female firefighter with long blonde hair. "You weren't supposed to be here today, were you, Ms. Marie? You don't dress like this to come to media day, except for Edward R. Murrow over there." He pointed at the young man that Captain Smith had helped get dressed.

Marie thought to say something funny, but she looked at Michael, "No, no, I wasn't, and I'll probably catch hell for it."

"Why did you come?" Michael asked.

Marie placed her hand on his arm. "I wanted to see you, Michael."

Michael was dumbfounded. He stepped back and sat down on the tailboard of the engine. "You wanted to see me?" Michael replied. He said again, "Me?" His mind was processing information at light speed, but nothing was making any logical sense.

Marie nodded and smiled slyly.

Michael sat back and said, "Marie, I have Friday off, but I know you have to do the news. Could you please go to dinner with me?"

"I get off at 10:30; I'll be out by 10:45. Just pick me up in front of the station."

Michael helped her get the rest of the turnout gear off. She reached up and gently kissed his cheek. "Gotta go." She walked over to Freddy, and they left. The smell of her perfume lingered in the air as Michael stood there still dumbfounded.

David was trying not to watch the whole event, but he did see the kiss. He went over to Michael and ran his hand in front of Michael's face. "Come on down to earth, Number 1. Did you get a date?"

"Yes!" Michael said. "Yes, I did."

"Look out, Chicago. Your most eligible bachelor just got bitten by the lovebug," David said, and they both laughed.

Chapter 11
An Unwelcome Homecoming

Mark was amazed at how well he was able to negotiate the TSA screening at the airport. He wasn't even given much of a second look by the agents. The passport and letter from the judge seemed to be exactly what the TSA agents needed, and soon Mark was sitting in business class sipping on a vodka and tonic. He flew from O'Hare International Airport to Germany.

The transfer in Germany was smooth, and sooner rather than later, he was on the ground in his small village of Ekazhevo. He was escorted to a small house on the outskirts of town by a member of the local militia.

Mark said, "Thank you." Mark handed the man a crisp United States one-hundred-dollar bill.

The gentleman nodded, and Mark knocked on the door.

"Enter," came a voice from inside.

Trial and Commitment

Mark stepped in, and sitting at the table was his father. The room had sparse furnishings and wooden floors. The furniture, what there was of it, was old and not well kept. The older gentleman was sitting on a chair at the kitchen table. He looked tired and weak, and it was obvious that he had not shaved or washed his clothes for a few days. There was no joy in his face when he saw Mark. This was not at all what Mark had imagined. His father had been a profitable businessman. He always dressed smartly, and he lived well. They never lacked for creature comforts, but it was clear to Mark that this broken man he observed at the table was not the gentleman that he had left years ago. It was clear to Mark that his father's experiences in the past few years were not pleasant.

Mark couldn't believe it. "I thought you were dead," Mark said.

"I am dead," the older gentleman said. "Dead to the world and dead to you."

"I wanted to come and see you," Mark said.

"You have seen me," the old man replied.

"The business?" Mark asked. "What of the business?"

"Gone."

"And Mother and Aysa?"

"Your mother died, and Aysa fled to the Russian Republic. I have not heard from her since," the old man replied. "I told her to go. Many of her age were taken by the radicals, and they never came home. They were raped or sold into slavery. Life is hard here; the radicals come from the south, they take what we have, and the government does not drive them out. They are murderers."

"I will come back for you, and we will leave together," Mark stated. Mark was enraged at what had become of his father, and he felt great pain when his father spoke of his mother and sister. He was moved to compassion as he realized that it had been his own doing that pulled him away from his family. There had been no celebration as he left for the United States, and there was no joy in his homecoming. He realized that he had let his family down. What if Aysa was dead too? He couldn't bear the thought of her being sold into the slave trade.

The old man looked intently at Mark. "I want to tell you a story," the old man continued. "I had a friend; he was a religious man, and he helped many here. He gave them food when they had none. He told me a story from his holy book about a young man who left his father and went away with his inheritance. When he left, a great famine came, and he lost all his money. To live, he had to live in filth with the pigs. *One day*, he thought, *I will go back to my father, and he will welcome me*. He told me that that was where you were but that you would come back to me. I think that you still live with the pigs, so how can I welcome you?" The old man's eyes were filled with tears.

"I do not live with the pigs anymore!" Mark replied. "I will return to take you with me."

"To where?" the old man asked. "To hell?"

Trial and Commitment

"I have been to hell," Mark replied. "I'm not going back there." He put some money on the table. "This is for you until I return, and I will find Aysa as well. Tell that to your holy man."

"He is dead, like all the rest," the old man stated. "Dead as I should be."

Mark left the house and headed back to the train station. He had a meeting in Beslan that he had to attend. It was time to get the job done and go home. The money was all that he cared about now.

Chapter 12
Date Night at the Hancock

Michael was not as nervous on the first day of academy as he was right now. His watch flashed the time: 10:46. He looked at door of the television station and back at his watch. He was parked near the Daley Plaza in front of the Channel 2 news station. Traffic was moving along the street, as the night was still young for Chicagoans. There were many people still at Daley Plaza, as the temperature was just right for spending the evening out-of-doors. He had been sitting there for ten minutes. His pickup truck was cleaned and even waxed, and there was a yellow rose sitting on the passenger seat. It was 10:48.

"Hey." Marie was standing by the front of the truck.

Michael jumped out of the truck to get to where she was. "I never even saw you come out the door."

"I came out the south doors," Marie said. "Should have told you, sorry."

He opened the door and handed her the rose.

"Nice. Thanks." She kissed him gently on the cheek. Michael's reaction to her kiss and her soft touch on his shoulder was nothing short of electric. He wanted to hold her close and kiss her again, but he knew that he had to be a gentleman.

"So where are we going?" she asked.

"To the Hancock. I know a really nice restaurant on the upper floor. It's a nice night. We can see the city," Michael said.

"Michael, I'm pretty much a down-to-earth kinda girl. You don't have to spend a lot of money to impress me; you already have," Marie said with a smile.

Michael was still in disbelief that this lady was in his truck. He almost expected himself to wake up from a dream. She was beautiful, and her every feature was exciting his deepest senses. "Nothing but the best for you," Michael said. "Besides, we already have reservations."

Marie looked at Michael. "Do you always tell the truth?"

"Yes, I certainly try to," Michael replied.

"Tell me what you were thinking when you first met me."

Michael thought, *This girl doesn't fool around; I'd better make this good.* "I thought that you were beautiful, smart, and way the hell out of my league!" Michael replied as they pulled up to the parking garage. Michael drove the truck up the ramps to the parking garage. It was late enough that many of the cars were gone, and they found a spot easily.

"Well, that just proves one thing," Marie said. "You're a good driver, but you aren't always right!"

"What do you mean by that?" Michael asked.

"I never thought you would be attracted to one of us bloodsucking media types, and I am not out of your league." Marie giggled and grabbed his hand, and they headed to the elevator.

Michael caught a slight whiff of Marie's perfume. *She is amazing!* he thought.

When they arrived at the restaurant, they noticed that there were not all that many diners. It was a clear night, and the city lights were radiant. *Perfect!* Michael thought.

"May I start you with something to drink, folks?" the waiter asked.

Marie looked at Michael, and Michael looked at Marie. *Well, here goes nothing*, Michael thought. "Something on draft?"

The waiter went through the litany of choices, but Michael was looking at Marie's eyes. *They are so dark*, he thought.

"Sir?" the waiter said. "Your choice?"

"Oh, uh, how about a dark beer, maybe an ale?" Michael asked.

"They don't have that on draft, silly," Marie said in a soft voice.

"Sorry. Something lighter, then, please."

"Sir, how about a nice light wheat beer?" The waiter smiled at him. "We have that."

"Sure, sorry," Michael said.

"She is a very beautiful lady, sir. It is all right." The waiter smiled again. "For you, ma'am?" the waiter said.

"I would like something light as well. May I have a glass of light white wine?"

"Yes, ma'am!" the waiter said. "Before I return, here is a list of appetizers, and I will be right back."

Michael said, "I'm surprised by one thing."

Marie looked intently at him. "And that would be?"

"That you aren't with some big, important high roller or other news guy."

"I deal with more egos than you can believe each day," Marie said. "'Is my hair okay?' 'Do I have enough makeup on?' 'Is the teleprompter keyed up?' 'Can I turn just a bit so the camera angle is better?' I get so tired of egos. I want a simple, real man, not an egomaniac." Marie smiled.

"Here are your drinks," the waiter said. "An appetizer, perhaps? The house special is shrimp, but I recommend the wings or some artichoke dip with a variety of crackers and bread."

Michael looked at Marie. Marie looked at Michael.

"Artichoke dip will be fine," Marie stated.

"Absolutely," the waiter said.

The dinner went on, and the two talked about various things. Marie asked Michael questions about his past and how he became a firefighter. Michael didn't mention medical school, and he was starting to relax.

When the check arrived, Michael opened the small leather case and looked at it. It was over one hundred dollars. *Wow*, Michael thought. *We had a few more drinks than I thought. Oh well.* He reached into his wallet for the credit card. Marie pulled out a hundred-dollar bill and set it on the table.

"No way, Marie," Michael said. "This is on me. Please."

"Look, Michael," Marie said, "you are a probationary firefighter, and I have an agent. You live in a small apartment, and I live downtown in an apartment that overlooks the lake. I want to help with this."

"Okay, well, then I get the meal, and you get the next stop, but we have to hurry if we want to make it," Michael said.

Marie put the money away.

"Please hurry with that," Michael told the waiter.

"I certainly will, sir."

As they pulled out of the parking garage, Michael drove south on Michigan Avenue to the river. It was 11:45. *Sure hope we make it*, he thought.

The boat tours had opened about two weeks previously for the spring season, and they just made the midnight cruise. As the ship passed down the river toward the lake, they passed under the Michigan Avenue Bridge. It was cool but not cold. Marie put her head on Michael's arm and held on to his arm tightly. "I was so nervous tonight I barely could read the newscast. I wanted so much for this night to go well."

Michael put his arm around her shoulders and asked her, "Well, how is it going?"

Marie looked at him and pushed toward him. Their lips met in a soft kiss. Michael closed his eyes and didn't open them for a few seconds. He felt a warmth and a feeling he had not felt for a very long time. It almost overwhelmed him.

"Are you all right?" she asked.

"Perfect!" Michael told her.

The boat passed quietly into Lake Michigan, and the skyline was bright, and the lights looked like diamonds in the reflection on the lake. Michael and Marie talked about their jobs, their lives, and the city. Marie was surprised to find out that Michael's father was a physician, but she didn't ask about it. Michael was just as surprised to find out that Marie was the daughter of a Mexican mother and an Irish father. *What a combination*, he thought.

After the cruise, they were in front of Marie's apartment. It was 1:30 a.m.

"Thanks again," Michael stated. "Can I please call you again?"

"Of course you can. I wouldn't have it any other way, but Michael, there is one thing that we have to do."

Michael looked at her. "I can barely wait for this one."

"I want to party with the firefighters one night! Can we please do that?"

"We can definitely do that," Michael said.

Michael walked Marie to the door where the night doorman met them and let Marie in. She grabbed a good-night kiss before she went it. "Good night, sweetie." And in she went!

Michael drove home in silence—no talk radio, no music. He had never been so ready for the rest of his life.

Chapter 13
Uranium and Cheese

Mark returned from his trip a day early, which pleased Simon and Nathan. Mark had been able to establish some contacts, and his desire to get the deal done and return to his homeland propelled him forward. Simon and Nathan had been eagerly awaiting his return.

"Fifteen kilograms—that's all I can secure," Mark said. "I was only able to get that because I assured them it would be intended for the primary target."

"Which is?" Nathan asked.

"Here in the United States," Mark replied. "That is what you are going to do with it? Correct?"

Both men looked at each other.

"Yes," Nathan said.

Simon looked at Nathan. "I would need more material to assure a true fissionable device. I don't know what the enrichment or the quality of the material might be. I don't think we can do what we need to do with fifteen kilograms of unknown material. I just can't be sure of the degree of enrichment."

Simon's career had led him from the United States Navy's atomic school through the prestigious University of Illinois's engineering program to a friend who was a nuclear engineer. All the while, the study of the construction and detonation of nuclear devices had intrigued him, but arms sales had been the more lucrative path to the life and wealth that he enjoyed.

"I can't get any more from anywhere," Mark continued. "The radicals are buying all of it, and who knows which government is buying the rest? What if you made contact with some of the people in the United States that could attempt to secure more?"

"It isn't that simple," Nathan answered. "We need it from a foreign country. That way, when the investigation is complete and we have used their Internet sites against them, this government will be convinced that the radicals have carried out the attack. These extremist groups will be blamed for the attack, and we can see to their destruction so that we can get back to the business that we enjoy."

"Why do you hate these people?" Mark asked. "Excuse my ignorance, but you don't seem to be the kind that would have prejudices toward these Islamic extremist organizations. They could be customers."

"Let's just say that we have had offers and dealings with these types of people, and they are not the kind of people that we respect or acknowledge. In fact, they need to be gone!" Nathan added.

"I still don't understand. What business other than importing all this cheese and pasta?"

Simon began, "I can tell you that we sold many items around the world before the radicals came to their so-called caliphate. They stole our wares, tried to kill our people, and destroyed our worldwide business."

"Armaments?" Mark asked. "Guns?"

"Not just guns but explosives, rockets, and other items that were in high demand and very lucrative to sell," Nathan stated.

"You didn't tell me you could bargain with arms," Mark stated.

"That is because we can't bargain with arms," Nathan replied. "That would expose us to the buyers and to the radicals. We have to buy the materials lucratively so we don't manifest ourselves as some extremist group that wants to get into the nuclear business. We cannot expose our company to any government or nongovernment scrutiny by any group that we—well, I mean *you*—deal with."

Mark asked, "You are using this to start a war?"

"Well, *war* is a relative term," Simon stated. "An attack by the United States with enough force to neutralize the threats from the radicals that have been destroying our business."

Simon looked intently at Mark and Nathan. "There is the other option to use the fissionable material to enhance the conventional explosives. The fingerprint of the radicals would be there, and we would have less exposure in building the device."

"I will inventory the supplies in the morning and see what we can do with what we have in stock in the high-order explosives cache," Nathan stated.

"So I have not cut the deal yet," Mark replied. "I wasn't sure how to get the materials here. You can't just put it in the carry-on compartment."

Simon wrote on a piece of paper and handed it to Mark. "Give them the name of this man in the Parma region of Italy, and he will work with them to get the materials and have them sent to us."

"How will it be sent here?" Mark asked.

"In cheese. Several separate containers," replied Simon. "Tell them we need it as soon as possible."

"I will get to work, but I need the secure server and the TracFones," Mark stated. "Please, if you would, let me get my account established. I could really use some money."

"Of course," stated Nathan, and Simon nodded in reply.

Chapter 14
A Night on the Town

Michael was sitting in his truck looking at a post that he had found on the news channel website.

It read:

Marie Kylie McCleary is the only child born of Mexican and Irish parents Shaun and Lucia. She grew up in Texas and attended both primary grades and high school in Brownsville. Ms. McCleary studied journalism at the University of Missouri at Columbia and began her career in Nashville at WVMQ covering the entertainment and traffic components of the news. She began her career in Chicago at the local CBS affiliate covering local news. She has quickly become a local favorite and covers news stories throughout the city.

Marie appeared at the door, and Michael went to meet her.

"Hey, handsome!" Marie greeted Michael.

"Hi, beautiful!" Michael replied, and they got into the truck and headed for a local pub where a few of the probationary firefighters and a few of the off-duty crews were getting together to watch the Bulls play the San Antonio Spurs. Michael always opened the door for Marie whether she was getting in or out of the truck.

"I'm a big girl, Michael. You don't have to do that," Marie told him.

"I don't have to, but I will," Michael replied.

Marie smiled and gave him a kiss

Several firefighters and their friends were in the sports bar already when the two walked in. Michael saw David at a table with his fiancée, Julie. They went over and sat down. Michael introduced Marie to Julie, and he went to the bar to get them each something to drink.

The conversation drifted from sports to the academy and what they had gone through together. Julie and David had gone through college as a couple and decided that they were going to get married before fall arrived. David had plans to ask Michael to be his best man.

"David helped me out a lot," Michael said. "He really showed me how to do what I needed to learn to be a firefighter."

"Were you a firefighter before CFD?" Marie asked David.

"Yep," David replied. "I was on a department in one of the South Suburbs."

"Why Chicago?" Marie asked.

"Gotta go where the action is!" David replied.

"He has it in his blood and in pictures all over the walls of the house and in the car, and I could go on!" Julie said, and they all laughed.

As the conversation continued, Marie kept looking intently at Michael each time he said something. She seemed to hang on his every word.

As Julie and Marie excused themselves from the table to go to the restroom, Julie asked Marie, "You really like Michael, don't you?"

Marie smiled. "Yes. I guess I was a little obvious."

"I stare at David like that too. It's all right, Marie," Julie said. "I asked David what you were like. Please don't take this the wrong way, but …"

"I know," Marie replied. "It's okay, Julie."

"No, no. I just mean that you are so down to earth."

"I feel down to earth when I am around him," Marie replied.

"Well, you made some new friends tonight," Julie told Marie, and she gave her a hug.

David and Michael started talking business after the girls left.

"You're pretty much the talk of the department," David told Michael. "People told me that they didn't know if you could put on the gear and perform when the time came, and I told them you would do it when you needed to, and you did."

"Thanks," Michael replied. "I'm still not sure how I did it. I just felt the foot, and before I knew it, Cliff was right there. It wasn't a textbook save, that's for sure, but we did it. You know that she came to see us at the station?"

"Really? What was that like?"

"Scary and awesome all rolled up into one," Michael said. "She could have died there. I was looking into the face of someone who could just as well have not been with the living anymore. Her eyes were so blue!"

"Who's eyes were blue?" Marie asked.

Michael and David had not noticed their return.

"Oh, the lady that we saved from the fire," Michael said. "She came to see us at the station."

"You saw her?" Marie asked.

"Yes, she came to visit us at the station, as I was just telling David."

"What was that like?" Marie asked.

"It was like I saw someone who could have been dead but she was alive—almost like I saw the effects of a miracle or something," Michael replied.

Julie said, "That had to be so rewarding."

"It was almost surreal," Michael said. "It was like watching myself meet her from across the room."

Marie and Michael watched the game, and then they decided it was time to go. Some of the other firefighters and their friends stayed at the bar.

As they were driving to Marie's apartment, Marie said, "Let's go and just sit by the lake for a while."

"Sure."

He drove to the parking lot near Montrose Beach. There weren't any cars in the lot. Michael put the truck in park and shut off the engine. Marie slid over in the seat and kissed him tenderly.

"How long have you known David?" she asked softly.

"I just me him in the academy," Michael told her. "We became instant friends."

"You'd follow him into a burning house?" Marie asked.

"There were days at the academy that I think I already have." Michael laughed.

Marie was holding Michael's hand and gently rubbing his arm.

"I have to admit that makes me just a bit jealous," Marie told Michael.

"There's no need to be. It's strictly a mutual-respect thing and a trust that you develop when you are with these people. When you are put in situations where you drop the defenses and just work for each other. It was like with Cliff in the apartment fire. He's a character, but he was there in a second when I yelled for help. It was really being part of a team," Michael said. "It's kinda why I did this."

Marie slid over and kissed him again.

Michael pulled Marie close to him and held her tightly. They held on for a long time.

As Michael let her gently slide back in the seat, he saw tears on her cheeks. "Hey, what's this about?" he asked as he gently wiped away a tear.

"Life wasn't so good in Nashville," she began. "I was young and impetuous and determined, and I landed a job with the station working as a traffic reporter, and then I started with the entertainment section. I got interviews—man, did I get interviews. But I soon realized it had more to do with my chest size than my ability to ask questions. Some of them actually looked me in the eyes." She smiled. "It was about not being taken seriously, I guess, but it paid well, and I did it. I met a guy who was with one of the bands. He was a great guitar player, and he liked me, and we got along well, or so I thought. He asked me to move in with him, and I did. He became very controlling and finally abusive. I tried to break away a few times, but he always promised that it would get better, and it did for a while, but …" She sobbed softly.

"It's all right," Michael whispered.

"Oh, Michael, it's not because you represent someone who has worked his tail off to get where you are and I … well, I compromised." She paused for a moment and wiped her eyes with a tissue that Michael had given her. "Anyway, I ended up in the ER one night after he had gotten drunk and hit me. A nurse got me some help, and so I stayed in a battered women's shelter for a week. Obviously, I quit my job, and I was determined that I was going somewhere where I would never compromise again. I sent a couple of interview demos out to Chicago and Dallas and Atlanta and landed the job here." Marie held Michael's hand tightly.

"I'm not what I thought I would be either," Michael told her. He relayed the story about how he had taken the academy test while he was applying for medical school.

"You mean you got in?" Marie asked.

"Yes, I was in, and that's exactly where I didn't want to be," Michael said. "So I headed for the academy, and here I am. Dad still isn't happy, and Mom, well, she knows I am destined to be what I am. And there was Katy." Michael paused and took a deep breath and cleared his throat.

"Before you go on," Marie said, "Cliff and I had a little talk at the fire academy on media day about that."

"Do you know Cliff?" Michael asked.

"No, not at all," Marie said. "He came up to me at the academy and said that he could see the way that I was looking at you and that he wanted to let me know that things were still tender. I told him I would respect that, and he said that he appreciated that. He told me that he was responsible for making you into a firefighter and wanted you to be happy. He also said that he liked you a lot even though you had only known each other for a couple of months. That's what I mean, Michael—it does make a girl somewhat jealous. You take care of each other."

"Well, at least you're smiling now," Michael said. "So where is this jerk, and has he ever contacted you?"

"No, oh no. He's off to another conquest," Marie said. "He was through with me and ready to move on."

"I'm so sorry," Michael whispered. "You never deserved anything like that."

"There's one more thing that you need to know, Michael," Marie said. "When I was in the shelter, I asked questions and thought a lot about my faith, which I had not thought about in a long time. I decided that I would think more of others than I did myself and try really hard to be more of a faith-filled person, and I feel better because of it. I don't worry about things in my future as much as I used to, and I am at peace spiritually."

Michael thought back to his days at Brother Rice High School and how he, too, had separated from his faith.

"We'll have to work on that too," Michael said. "I've been part of a miracle!"

"You mean finding the lady?" Marie asked.

"Yes, and that too," Michael said. "I was talking about when you said hi to me."

Marie looked in Michael's eyes. "There is one more thing."

"What's that?"

"I'm falling hard, and I swore that I would not do this again for a long, long time," Marie said.

"I'll catch you," Michael whispered in her ear.

Marie kissed Michael again, and they held each other for a bit longer before Michael drove her home.

Chapter 15
The Picture

Agent Brian Lattis was reviewing his e-mail and looking at the intelligence reports on the movement of known arms dealers and potential weapons of mass destruction threats. *Nothing, nothing, nothing. Such goes the way of an intelligence analyst*, he mused. *Wait a minute*, he thought. *I know this guy.*

Agent Lattis was second-generation Federal Bureau of Investigation. His father had been with the bureau for many years, and Brian followed in his father's footsteps after an attempt at a pro baseball career. He had enjoyed his tenure with the bureau, graduating in the top 10 percent of his class just five years earlier. His passion was studying about terrorism and terrorist-related activities, and he had become part of the Chicago Joint Terrorism Task Force (JTTF) two years earlier.

In front of him was a grainy photograph at an airport in Grozny. It showed two individuals talking. One of the individuals had been tagged as someone of interest that may have been involved in smuggling activities involving potential weapons that could be used for mass destruction attacks. The individual was tagged by the Foreign Intelligence Service of the Russian Federation.

Agent Duncan Furgeson was standing on the other side of the room talking to a coworker.

"Hey, Duncan," Brian said. "Come over and look at this picture for a minute, would you, please?"

Duncan made his way over to the computer. Duncan Furgeson had served in an exchange program between the FBI and the British MI5 agency. Duncan had returned to be part of the FBI once his exchange program had ended. Duncan liked living across the pond, and the bureau had quickly offered him a job. He had also worked closely with intelligence agencies in Israel and Greece.

"This guy here," Lattis said, "not the one that they have tagged, but the other one. Does he look familiar to you?"

Duncan Furgeson studied the image closely. "He sure looks like he doesn't belong there."

"Why do you say that?"

Furgeson pointed at the jacket. "Looks like he's from the West. Clothes don't fit in."

Lattis hadn't noticed that, but he had to admit his friend was right. "I think I know him," he said.

"Any idea from where?"

"That I don't know," said Lattis. "I'm going to see if our computer personnel can clean this up a bit. I want to see this guy's face a bit better."

Lattis picked up the phone and dialed the computer lab.

"We need a day or two, Agent Lattis," the technician said. "We can probably clean it up a bit, but I'll have to see how the pixelation works out."

"Thanks," Lattis answered.

Furgeson asked, "Do you think you know this guy? Do you have an idea that this guy's up to something?"

"Aren't they all?" replied Lattis. "I might be looking for a needle in a haystack."

Chapter 16
Delivery

Nathan and Simon were at the warehouse when the five large containers of fontina cheese arrived on the trucks. Each container was mixed with other types of cheese that had been packaged a few days before by workers in Italy. The transfer had gone smoothly, as there had been an extra fifty thousand paid to the Italians to be sure that all went well.

"This is by far the most expensive cheese we have ever bought," Nathan said as the cheese was unloaded and stored in a cooler in the warehouse.

"It will be worth it to get the material," Simon replied.

"What of Magomed?" Nathan replied. "He has been acting strangely and keeping to himself."

"He is concerned over his father and sister, I think," Simon replied.

"He was paid well," Nathan said. "Perhaps it is time he was relieved of his duties and allowed to go back to Chechnya."

"Not quite yet," replied Simon. "He may still serve our needs. He is a lost soul looking to find some absolution for his past sins. He may yet be able to help us."

Nathan greeted a man that had just entered the building. He was a smaller man whose slight appearance made him look somewhat feeble.

"I'm sure you remember Mr. B," Nathan told Simon. "He is our friend that we have brought into our services. He has quite a bit of training in conventional and high-order explosives."

Mr. B. was Alan Buchanter. Mr. B., like Mark, was released from prison when Simon's lawyer, Mr. Peterson, looked closely into his case and was able to secure his release on lack of evidence by the prosecution after a judge looked at the information presented in the case.

Simon greeted Mr. B. "It has been a while, my friend. Glad to see that you are doing well!"

"Thanks, Simon, and good to see you as well. How much of the C-4 derivative were you able to secure?" Mr. B. asked.

"Enough to be sure that the fissile material can be sufficiently disseminated," Nathan stated.

"What is the delivery vehicle?" Mr. B. asked.

"One of our delivery trucks, like this one." Nathan pointed to a large one-ton delivery truck with the company logo on the side.

"The suspension will need to be beefed up," Mr. B. said. "We need to be sure the materials are in a lead-lined vault, and I'll probably fill it with an absorptive material like paraffin so that the materials are not detectible while you are moving. There are a lot of detection devices around the city on any given day. The last thing you want is to have some overenthusiastic cop or roadway employee getting a nuclear read on this truck."

"Can you work on that as well?" Nathan asked.

"I suppose so," Mr. B. said. "It'll take more time. I thought this was a hurry-up operation."

"We have some time," Nathan answered. "Not a lot of time, but we have some time."

"And just so that I have this straight," Mr. B. asked, "you want this to look like something that those radical characters from the Middle East put together?"

"Exactly."

"They're simple operators," Mr. B. said with a disgruntled look on his face. "They don't get their detonators from reliable sources, and you gotta be damn careful; otherwise, things go *boom* before they are supposed to. We can make it look that way, except for the truck. You gotta rent one; otherwise, they find parts of this one, just like they did in Oklahoma City, and you boys are smack-dab in the middle of all this."

"Understood," Nathan stated. "It will be done."

"Now, let's see the explosives so I can start thinking about how we want to do this."

Mr. B. and Nathan left the building to go to another warehouse. Simon left as well for a meeting that he had in Chicago. Simon reflected on his relationship with Nathan as he drove. Theirs was more than a partnership. He deeply cared for Nathan.

Chapter 17
A Distraction

Mark entered his code and walked into the warehouse that they called Warehouse 2. He recognized the man that he had been introduced to that they called Mr. B.

"Where are Simon and Nathan?" Mark asked.

"They were here this afternoon," Mr. B. said. "They left about three hours ago. Are you looking for them?"

"No, not really," replied Mark. "I was looking for a schedule for the delivery to Indianapolis that is supposed to happen in the next couple of days."

"That one's not in my wheelhouse," Mr. B. replied. "But since you are here, let me show you something."

Mark nodded and went over to where Mr. B. was standing.

"It is very important to understand that these will be shaped charges and that most of the fissile materials will be ejected toward the passenger side of the vehicle. So it is important that they park with that side of the truck facing the building."

"I will not be driving," said Mark. "I will be sure that whoever it is knows what you have said."

Mr. B. finished installing the heavy steel plate behind the charges and turned to look at Mark. "I have to get a shower before I go, as we don't want any of this material to get out of the building. Most of these response vehicles are carrying some type of radioactive detection device. Now whether the fire cats and coppers know how to use them is a different story."

"Do you have the uranium in the charges now?" Mark asked.

"No," said Mr. B. "It'll go in the day before we deploy this truck."

"How much longer will it take?" Mark asked.

"Couple of more days, but Simon will determine when we actually send it out," Mr. B. said. "You don't know a lot about these people, do you?"

"No," Mark answered.

"Well, if you'll give me few minutes," Mr. B. said, "I'll walk over to this little bar down the street, and I'll buy you a drink. You Russian fellows do drink, don't you?"

"I'm actually from Chechnya," answered Mark. "Yes, we do drink. Vodka here and there has been known to cure many ills."

"Or start new ones," Mr. B said, and they both laughed. "I'll meet you down the street."

Mark walked down the street and sat down. The bartender came over, and Mark ordered a drink. She looked at Mark intently and said, "You look like a man who has a lot on his mind tonight."

"You really wouldn't believe it if I told you," Mark told the bartender. She was a tall brunette that, as Mark had observed on a previous trip, was easy to look at.

"Maybe you should tell me sometime." She smiled at Mark.

"Perhaps we can arrange that," Mark said. "Right now, I have to go see the gentleman that just walked in."

Mr. B. and Mark sat at a table in the back of the bar away from the other patrons.

"You cannot be too careful in this city," Mr. B. told Mark.

"I would like to know more about who I am working for," Mark said.

"Well, first off, these are the nicest bunch of patriots that you could ever want to work for or meet. They have treated me well. I was in prison, like you, and they used their attorney to find inconsistencies in the prosecution's case against me and worked for my release. I am a demolition specialist by trade. I learned the skill early in the United States Army. Uncle Sam taught me the business of ordnance."

"How long were you in the army?" Mark asked.

"Well, now, that, too, is part of the problem. See, I wanted to stay in and just build and study ordnance all my life, but there were a couple of high-ranking officers that I just couldn't see eye to eye with—including a certain major named Malloy who took it upon himself to see to it that the United States Army and I parted ways. We did, and I left with a dishonorable discharge for insubordination. And, of course, Malloy now works for the City of Chicago, so this delivery has a personal appeal to me."

Mark looked at Mr. B. "Sorry to hear that."

"Well, I was too, but I thought I'd just stay in the trade that I knew," continued Mr. B. "Do you know how many civilian ordnance jobs you can get with a dishonorable discharge?"

Mark shook his head.

"None, ничегоnye!" answered Mr. B. "You are damaged goods. So I went to be a mechanic, but I still dabbled in the business and even did some jobs. Nothing in the jobs that I did was below the board, mind you, just some timber-clearing operations and some building demolition. Then I met this guy who needed some explosives to put a scare into some people. How was I to know he was out to whack his ex? And he did it—he brought the whole house down on her, and I was an accomplice, so off to the big house I go. That's when I got out and met Nathan and Simon."

"The lawyer—is he part of the operation?"

"Nope, not from what I gather," answered Mr. B. "He's in it for the bucks. Imagine that, a lawyer in it for the bucks!"

They both laughed.

"He just wants enough money to head to some South American country where he can lie low for a while and then return to the States. He has the right idea, but I'm thinking Argentina, and I find some nice gal with a couple of kids that needs some help and I can settle down."

Mark felt confident that Mr. B was on the up-and-up. Mark had learned to be a good judge of who people were and how sincere they might be. He went further with his questions.

"Why this bomb? Why this plan?"

"The radicals—we call them that because there isn't, in my opinion, a nickel's worth of difference between them," Mr. B. said. "All they want to do is battle with everyone and kill as many 'infidels' as they can. They are barbarians. Well, anyway, sorry—got off the topic. They wanted some arms, so Nathan and Simon worked through some people in Lebanon or one of those countries to sell them some arms, so long as they not be used against our troops or US interests, and they agreed. Simon believed them. Their real plan was to steal the arms, do away with Simon and Nathan, and be gone. They wanted to deal directly with Simon, so he went, and thankfully we all encouraged them not to trust anyone and wear a Kevlar vest. The car they were in took some rounds, and Simon was damn near killed."

"Why did they want to kill him?"

The bartender stood by Mark and asked if they would like another drink. Mr. B. nodded, and the bartender went to get the drinks.

Mr. B. looked at Mark. "Guess she likes your type."

"She talks to me a lot when I am in here," Mark said.

The bartender walked back with the drinks and put them on the table, smiled, and picked up the twenty-dollar bill.

"Keep the change, darlin'," Mr. B. said.

The bartender smiled at them and walked away.

"Where were we? Got distracted," Mr. B. said. "Oh yeah. I don't know why they wanted to kill either of them—maybe competition. Who knows? Like I said, they are barbarians. They know no bounds when it comes to hate and destruction. So you build a bomb and make it look like these radicals detonated it, and maybe somebody in the Big House will decide to go after these jerks and wipe them out or at least beat them back to the nineteenth century so we can get back to the business that we do."

Mark's thoughts turned to the building. *There will be innocents*, he thought. For some unknown reason, he remembered his chance encounter with the firefighter a few days earlier. *He will die too*, he thought.

Mr. B. and Mark visited a while longer and then shook hands and parted ways. Mark walked to the bar to have just another drink before he departed.

The bartender walked over to Mark. "Did your friend leave?"

"Yes," Mark answered. "I think he has an early day tomorrow."

"And what about you?" she asked.

"I'm just kind of in hold mode right now," Mark answered. "May I buy you a drink?"

"I thought you'd never ask," the bartender replied.

Mark smiled.

"My name is Maggie," the bartender said, "and I like your accent."

"I was born in Chechnya," Mark told her, "and I moved to the area a few years ago."

"What do you do?"

"I am a buyer," Mark answered. "I work at the import company down the street. Maggie, I think you like being a bartender."

Maggie replied, "I do like bartending. I feel as though I am doing something that people like. I've always thought that I am personable, and even though I don't consider myself to be pretty, I do receive compliments occasionally. They make me feel good. I decided that just because I turned forty last year, I didn't have to look forty, so I have been working out for over a year now."

Mark looked intently at Maggie. "I have liked seeing you in the last few weeks. That is why I come back."

Maggie told Mark that she had been part of a failed marriage and her ex-husband had decided that she and her eight-year-old son, Aden, were a burden, and he had disappeared soon after they divorced.

"I'm sorry to hear that," Mark replied.

Maggie said, "I really didn't want to work, but I needed the money to help raise Aden, and quite frankly, bartending pays pretty darned well when you include tips. I have been here for over a year, and the owner wants me to stay, so he offered me a raise six months ago and one just last week. I also help the girls learn the business, and I have even given a few of them some money to help them out till they get paid.

"So how long have you worked for the buyer?"

"Only a few weeks," Mark replied. "You seem different from the rest of the girls. Not as impetuous."

Maggie smiled. "I just want to raise my son and make people happy."

"You have made me happy tonight just by talking to me."

"You're not American, that's for sure. You say what you think. Most American guys play games."

Mark smiled at her. "I don't know how to play games." He thought, *What is going on with you? You're in this for the money and to return home. Don't get so friendly with her.*

"I get off in thirty minutes. Do you want to walk with me to the park down the street? It is a nice night." She couldn't believe she had just asked this guy to walk with her.

Mark looked at Maggie, and she was looking at him with her dark eyes. *I can't believe how beautiful this girl is*, he thought.

"Yes, I will walk with you," he said, and he smiled.

The walk with Maggie was one of the nicest times he had had in America. They talked about their lives—though with Mark, certain things were excluded. Maggie talked about her son and what she had been through. They talked for over an hour on the bench in the small park by Maggie's apartment.

This isn't supposed to be happening, Mark kept telling himself.

He didn't even kiss her when they parted. They just exchanged a hug and went their separate ways. Mark thought about Maggie the entire evening and all the next day.

Chapter 18
The Intuition

Agent Brian Lattis looked intently at the image that had been enhanced by their photo laboratory personnel. "I think we need to see where else this face has appeared," he told his boss.

Special Agent in Charge Robert Nettles looked intently at Lattis. "Brian, if you think this is something that will lead somewhere, we will do it, but the last few haven't been what I would call showstoppers."

"I have a pretty strong feeling that this guy has crossed our path before," Lattis told his boss.

"Before we get this thing analyzed to the nth degree, send this to STIC in Springfield."

STIC is the Statewide Terrorism & Intelligence Center. STIC is a fusion center to share information both within the geographical limits of the state and around the country. It is staffed by analysts that can analyze and compare intelligence information from several

Trial and Commitment

law enforcement and Homeland Security sources. The information is usually about suspicious activities or individuals that may have been involved in activities that might be law enforcement related or just generally strange enough to merit an investigation of one sort or another. STIC is located in Springfield.

Agent Lattis shared the photo with STIC so that he could verify the content of the photo and see if the mystery man was someone that he had crossed paths with before.

Chapter 19
Trial by Fire

"Where's Captain Smith?" Michael asked as the shift began.

"He got into one of those national incident management classes in the academy this week," Cliff said. "They had some openings, and he applied and got in."

"What's he learning?" Michael asked.

"They teach them how to manage disaster response and all about incident management," DJ answered.

"David said he took one of those classes when he was in the burbs," Michael said.

"He took it on purpose?" Cliff asked.

"Yes. Said it was dry, but the instructors kinda made it fun. He said they were from the fire institute in Champaign," Michael replied.

"Fun?" Cliff said. "Besides, nothing big ever happens in Chicago." He smiled. "That's why they pay the FDNY guys so much. They take all the heat for us with this terrorism business."

"How's the relationship going?" Cliff asked. He said it with a big smile.

Michael looked at Cliff and DJ, who were figuratively salivating for some juicy details. "She's one of a kind."

Cliff rolled his eyes. "He's whipped already." He got up from his chair to go to the bay and begin safety checks on the engine.

"You would be too if she were with you, Mr. Cliff Casanova," DJ said, and he slapped Michael on the back. "She's hot!"

"Boys, boys, boys," Michael said, and he followed them to the bay. Michael laughed to himself. *She is one of a kind*, he thought.

The captain for the shift was a floater who had recently been promoted and traveled all over the city until he received a permanent assignment.

DJ looked at Michael as they left for the bay. "This captain has been with special operations before his promotion. He's a no-nonsense kind of person."

The three decided they would make it a low-key day.

The checks went without a hitch, and the first call was to a van on its side on the interstate near the University of Illinois at Chicago.

When they arrived, there were already two ambulances on scene.

Cassie was there with one of the ambulances. She walked up to Cliff. "This is a real mess. We gotta cut her out. The semi mangled the car pretty good. He switched lanes and took out the passenger side of the vehicle. I need somebody with gear to get into the car with her, so send Michael over to the van."

The captain went over to where she was standing. "Hi, Cassie. What do you need?"

"Let me have the kid with me and my crew. He has some medical training, and I could use him."

"Okay, Cassie," the captain replied. "Firefighter Fortenier—with this lady, please."

"Yes, sir," Michael said, and he followed Cassie.

"I'll have no idea how badly she is hurt till we get to her. I think her right leg is screwed up pretty good," Cassie said.

Michael was always impressed at the way she carried herself in the field. *If she were a guy, she would be a stud!* he thought.

The car was on its top, and the lady that Cassie referred to was pinned in the car. As the firefighters in the squad truck that had accompanied Michael's team to the scene readied their rescue equipment, Michael gently crawled through the back window and into the van with the lady.

"My name is Michael, and I am here to help you," he said.

The lady looked at him. "I can't feel my legs," she replied. "Am I going to die? I feel like I am going to die."

"We are going to get you out of here," Michael told her. "It is going to get kinda noisy in here for a while. They are going to cut the car away from you."

"Oh, it hurts! My back hurts." She began to cry. "Please don't let me die, please."

"Just relax as much as you can," Michael told her as he checked her vital signs. He felt like he and the lady and the space they were in were the only things in the world even though the other responders were just inches away. The outside world seemed so distant. The car and the lady were the only things in Michael's world right now, and that's when the feeling hit him. He had been here before on an icy highway in a van, but that time he was being rescued. Michael experienced a feeling that came over him like a wave. *Maybe I was supposed to be here all along.*

His flashback was short-lived as he was snapped back to reality.

"Michael, give me the vitals." It was Cassie. She was right near the front window.

"Pulse is ninety and kinda thready," Michael told her. The term *thready* is sometimes used to describe a rather weak pulse.

"Respirations?" Cassie asked.

"Thirty plus," Michael replied.

"She's going into shock. C'mon, boys, let's get her outta here!" Cassie said to the firefighters who were stabilizing the vehicle.

One of the firefighters on the squad said, "We're going to lay the top over and see what we got from there."

Michael recognized the firefighter as Walt. He was from another station.

"Tell me about your family," Michael encouraged the lady. He was trying to get her to relax.

"My husband is a doctor at Rush. We have two children, and I'm pregnant with the third. Oh, please get me out of here," she said.

"Cas, she's pregnant," Michael said.

"What?"

"She's pregnant," Michael told her again.

The firefighters had just completed cutting the pillars, which were the support posts between the top of the van and the body of the van, and were folding the top down. Michael gently supported the woman's head as the top of the van was folded down like opening a door.

"We need some fluids, now!" Cassie told her partner. Cassie and Michael were both in the car now that the top of the car had been folded down. Cassie was prepping the lady's hand for the IV.

"Her leg is in there pretty good," Walt said. "We are going to have to jack the car to free her. Buy me some time, Cassie."

"We don't have a lotta time, Walt," Cassie replied.

Michael helped Cassie with the IV and held the IV bag as Cassie started the IV and the fluids began to flow.

"How far along are you?" Cassie asked the lady.

"Three months," the lady replied. "My back is getting numb now."

"How long have we been here?" Cassie asked the captain.

"Ten minutes on the extrication," he replied.

"C'mon, boys, we gotta go!" Cassie said to the firefighters. "We are eating into the golden hour."

"We got it jacked now, Cas," Walt replied. "We're cutting the floor out now."

Michael knew exactly what was going on. This was a race against time that they were losing.

"Can you get another IV in, Cassie?" Michael asked.

"Give me another start kit," Cassie said to her partner.

"Is your name Cassie?" the lady asked.

"Yep, that's me," Cassie replied.

"My husband knows you," the lady said. "He is Dr. Randle, and he works in the ER sometimes."

"He's a good man," Cassie replied. "I'll bet you can't wait—"

Walt spoke to Cassie and cut off her conversation. "We are about to get her leg out, but we will need some pressure dressings. Lotta blood here."

Cliff and another firefighter were bringing supplies to the paramedics.

There were two more paramedics on scene, as another ambulance that was en route from the hospital back to quarters stopped to help. "What do you need, Cas?" one of them asked.

"We gotta get the leg bandaged as soon as they free it, and I mean fast!" Cassie replied.

Michael had seen his share of injuries, as he had done some clinical rotations in his last year of college, but this was by far the worst injury that he had been exposed to. It was a compound fracture, which meant that the bones of the lower leg were exposed, but there was very much tissue damage as well, and the foot was limp and had no muscle tone.

The medics gently wrapped the extremity in trauma dressings. Cliff and another firefighter had the stretcher at the car, so all they had to do was get the patient onto a long spine board to immobilize her back and neck and then onto the stretcher.

Cassie was on the phone. "Yeah, she will need to go to surgery. I'm telling you now that is what you will need to be ready

Trial and Commitment

for. It's almost cut off. Yeah, the foot. Okay, thanks, babe." Cassie was talking to a trauma nurse that she knew well.

Michael helped get the patient to the ambulance. She looked pale and weak, not the same lady that he had talked with ten minutes earlier. The other ambulance that had come to the scene took the transport. As Cassie shut the doors, the ambulance left for Rush University Medical Center.

"Your dad there today?" Cassie asked Michael.

The fact that Michael's father was head of surgery had absolutely escaped from his mind at that moment.

"I think so," Michael replied. He looked intently at Cassie. "How do you do it, each day, every day?"

Cassie looked intently at Michael and put her hand on his arm. Michael was seeing a side of his mentor that he had not experienced before. "You rely on the people you know and trust. They get you through it."

"Do you think she will …" Michael stopped short.

"I don't know. She lost a lot of blood." Cassie patted Michael on the back. "Hang in there, Michael. You will be all right." She walked over to the squad and gave Walt and his crew a hug. "Thanks, Walt!"

"Anytime, Cas," Walt responded.

Michael was beginning to understand what it all meant as he looked up and saw the man standing there. Mark had been behind the van on the interstate and had seen the whole crash take place. He had stopped to see what the problem was. He walked up to the fire engine that was on the scene and had seen the whole extrication take place. As Michael walked away from Cassie, Mark raised his hand to wave at him.

Michael walked over to Mark. "We have met before."

They shook hands.

"Yes," Mark replied. "We met at the roast beef restaurant. That must have been very stressful."

Michael looked down. "The paramedics that we work with are very good at what they do."

"You are very modest," Mark said. "You are a firefighter that should be proud of what you do. You help people, and that is a very good thing. I wish you well."

"Thanks again," Michael said. "What did you say your name was again?"

"Magomed, but my friends call me Mark."

"Good luck to you as well, Mark." Michael gave Mark a last glance and smiled as he walked toward the engine.

"Who was that?" DJ asked Michael.

"Just a guy I met at the roast beef restaurant," Michael said. "Probably just a guy who ended up in the wrong place at the right time."

Chapter 20
Tying Things Together

Brian Lattis looked closely at the e-mail that he had received from the intelligence analyst at STIC.

It included the following information, which Lattis read aloud:

Magomed Domechian was released from Stateville Correctional Center as a result of a judge's order because of inconsistencies in the prosecutorial evidence presented at his case. He received a visa to travel to visit an ailing relative in Chechnya a week later and was out of the country for a few days. There were no inconsistencies in his travel reports. He met with no one except his ailing father in Ekazhevo. There has not been another trial scheduled.

Lattis looked at Furgeson. "Well, they missed this one. What did the Russians say about this guy he seems to have met with?"

Duncan Furgeson was looking at the report. "He is an alleged dealer of armaments and probably other weapons. That is all it says." Furgeson was communicating with one of his associates in the Foreign Intelligence Service. The Russian agent and Agent Furgeson had met a few years before in Greece, and despite the language barrier, they seemed to hit it off well.

"Weapons of mass destruction—do you think this might involve radioactive material that seems to keep popping up from time to time?"

"The report doesn't say that," Furgeson said. "I think the Russians are trying to secure as much of it as they can since we convinced them that they are as much of a target as anyone else is."

"I'd say they didn't get all the material," Lattis continued. "I wonder who would have decided to spring this guy and why." He studied the material provided by IDOC. "Well, son of a gun, if it isn't our friend attorney Lawrence Peterson who came to the rescue again. And IDOC says that Mr. Domechian is working at the Midwest Wine and Cheese Importers as a buyer and warehouse staff."

"So maybe we should talk with Mr. Domechian?" Furgeson asked.

"You know, maybe we should just have some of the agents look the Midwest Wine and Cheese Importers warehouse for a day or so and just see what we have going on there," Lattis said. "I'll see if I can get the boss to let us take a look."

"You know he is always willing to work with you." Duncan Furgeson was being sarcastic. "You really don't have anything else on this guy except that he was in a foreign country, and he ended up having his picture taken with a suspected arm dealer at the wrong time." Furgeson smiled and flashed his badge at Lattis. "Maybe we should just do it ourselves."

"Yes, maybe we should, Duncan. I'll start the paperwork."

Chapter 21
Dinner

Michael was busy about the process of cleaning his apartment. This was the first official visit by a female to his apartment since Katy had been there.

Marie assured him that she was comfortable with his living arrangements, but Michael was absolutely sure that there were some things that women implied that were not true, so his cleaning had begun two hours earlier, and he was through vacuuming, and now the dusting and tidying up was in full swing.

There were two steaks marinating in the refrigerator, and he had purchased salad and potatoes and even some vegetables that he was preparing for the dinner. He was really a decent cook and was pretty proud of some of the meals he'd made at the fire station. The payoff at the fire station was that the cook didn't have to do dishes.

Michael took a shower and was ready for Marie's arrival at 5:30. She had taken the evening off to be with him.

As Marie arrived, Michael's heart skipped a beat. He had contemplated this evening for the past few days, and his inability to concentrate on the firehouse discussion was readily apparent to his friends.

The day before, DJ asked Michael, "What's with you? You sick?"

Cliff joined in, "He is sick, all right. Lovesick!"

Michael wrinkled his nose and looked at him. "I'm just *pensive*."

"Pensive?" Cliff asked. "I didn't learn that in the academy." Cliff laughed and jabbed Michael in the arm.

"Okay, so I'm cooking dinner for the two of us tomorrow night. I can't keep anything from you characters," Michael said.

"Ooooh, wow," Cliff said, and he laughed.

"You guys are killing me," Michael said.

They razzed him the rest of the day.

Marie was dressed in jeans and a red blouse that made Michael's eyes just about pop out of his head.

"Wow," was all he could get out as he opened the door.

Marie smiled. "Hello, honey!" She kissed him, and they hugged each other tenderly.

Michael gently kissed her on the neck.

She playfully spun away from him. "Hey, now, I think we have to cook."

"It's done," Michael told her.

"What?" she said as she walked into the dining room. "Smells like air freshener. How long have you been cleaning?"

"Not long. Not long at all."

Marie looked at him.

"Okay, for a couple of hours," he said. "I wanted it to look nice for you."

Marie kissed him again. "You're sweet!"

Marie and Michael walked into to the kitchen, and they brought the food to the dining room. Michael also had purchased a bottle of wine that the lady at the wine store told him would go best with dinner.

They talked about what their week had been like as they ate. *Funny*, Michael thought, *I've never felt uncomfortable when we are together.*

They finished the bottle of wine and placed the dishes in the sink.

"I'm washing these," Marie said, and she started the water in the kitchen sink.

Trial and Commitment

"I can do it later," Michael said.

"Honey, you don't get this yet," Marie told Michael. "This is the best part, when we do things together. Cook together and, yes, even wash the dishes together. I love the simple things."

Michael had never had so much fun washing the dishes. Marie rolled up her sleeves and accomplished her domestic chore with a flair that left him in amazement.

After they had completed the dishes and cleaned up the leftovers, they went to sit on the couch.

Marie looked at Michael. "I've been so nervous about tonight."

Michael looked at Marie. "Why? You seem so calm and collected whenever I am around you."

"This is a new world for me, Michael. I've never been treated like this. The last relationship was unstable at best. I rarely cooked, and we rarely spent time together unless he needed something that he felt I could give him. Then he took what he wanted and went to bed. At the office, I am treated differently. I have an agent, and I make more money than the other reporters do. That puts me in a class that they think makes me different from them. I try hard not to be that way, but it doesn't seem to work. I get along with them, and I like Freddy and the others that I work with, but it's the culture of the business. I've tried to change it, but I finally just gave up and live with it."

"And the fact that you are extremely beautiful," Michael said.

"I don't think of myself that way," Marie said. "Sometimes my perceived looks work against me. People don't approach me like I wish they would. I get tired of being treated like a porcelain doll and just wish people would take me for what I am."

Michael and Marie sat in silence for a few minutes. Michael was running his fingers through her long, dark hair. She laid her head back and kissed him. Michael was overcome by the moment and her beauty. His hands were caressing her warm body.

Marie moved herself closer to Michael, and things were getting intense when she realized that she was about to lose clothing. She stopped and looked into Michael's eyes. "We can't do this just yet."

Michael sat back and took a deep breath. "Okay," he said.

"It's not like I don't want to," she whispered to him. "I just want to be sure that we do this the right way. You have no idea how much I want to surrender to you right now."

"You know, honey, it's so incredible just to be with you. You are so kind to me, and you are so beautiful, and I just—"

She put her finger over his lips. "Shhhhhhhh."

They held each other closely. The food and wine had taken its toll, and they both relaxed.

Marie woke up at 1:00 a.m. still in Michael's arms.

"I gotta go home, honey," she said. "I gotta go in early."

Chapter 22
A Change Is Coming

Mark woke up in a cold sweat. He looked at the clock near his bed. It was 3:00 a.m.

Another horrible dream again.

Mark was standing in front of his father, and the words were being said by his father again: "I think that you still live with the pigs, so how can I welcome you?" He saw his father's face clearly, and his tears were real.

In a dream the night before, he had seen Aysa's face. She was on her knees with a man dressed in black behind her. She had been taken captive and was being sold as part of the human trafficking in a Middle Eastern country. He could see her face so clearly. She cried out to him for help, and the man behind her grabbed her and dragged her away into another room. Her screams ... how real. How he wanted to get to her, but he couldn't.

And the night before that, it had been the faces of people screaming in pain as the bomb exploded near the government building. They were real people, not faceless, lifeless victims. The screaming was so loud, and the pain they felt seared into Mark's emotions.

And the night before that, it had been the young firefighter and his team running into the burning building. Mark distinctly heard the young firefighter say, "We're just firefighters. It's what we do."

This was not at all what he wanted or hoped for.

Alcohol and sleep aids had not helped. Same dreams night after night …

Mark was having some very strange ideas about the whole situation. Nathan and Simon had been very good to him, but this idea of a dirty bomb was causing him more and more distress. This was not something he was happy with at all.

Mark thought back on his life and how his focus had been on money and living the good life when there really had been no good life. Narcotics had been an easy life at first, but then as he got deeper and deeper into the business, there was always the idea that you were being followed. The police were around every corner, and the betrayers were always something to worry about. Would the deal go bad? Would the undercover agents infiltrate the system? There were always questions, and when he actually thought that he had had enough money to live comfortably, he had been betrayed by those that he had helped. They had sold him out to the police, and the only comfort that he had was that they had been taken down in the process.

Prison had been something out of a bad movie. He had been caught between two rival gangs in the penitentiary. He could not buy protection, and as he refused to align with gangs. He had been hated by them all. There was the shank to the leg and the broken ribs and the thought of ending it all just to be away from it.

Nathan and Simon were good to him. Money was plentiful, and there was the thought that he was comfortable for the first time in a long time, but once the bomb was detonated, he would be a wanted man of the highest order if anything went wrong.

Mark was stretched between emotions of all kinds, and the dreams didn't help.

He was no hero, he was no savior, but he was also no terrorist, and that was what he was quickly becoming.

Chapter 23
Realization

Mark and another member of the team returned from Indianapolis at about 5:00 p.m. They had taken a load of cheese to a rental facility in Indianapolis. The "cheese" was actually boxes of guns and ammunition that had been stored at the Chicago facility. The only thing that Mark had been told was that the commodities were being moved so that they would not be found.

Mark knew the reality of their move; the Chicago operation was being vacated, and everyone in the company that had any knowledge of what was to come was soon going to fade into the proverbial woodwork.

Chechnya had been his dream; Chechnya was to be his salvation. It was half a world away where he could forget all this. It was a place where he could live alone with his father and Aysa. He knew he could find Aysa if he just had the chance. Emotions were not something Mark knew or appreciated, but suddenly they were appearing.

He opened the door to the bar and walked in.

She smiled as she saw him come in.

Mark entered into a place that was foreign to him. Certainly not the bar, certainly not the atmosphere, but into a place where a beautiful woman smiled at him as though she were glad to see him. This was new, and Mark had to admit that his defenses began to drop.

Maggie brought Mark a drink, his favorite imported vodka. "How was the trip?" she asked.

"A long drive and a long day," Mark said.

Mark noticed that Maggie had on an outfit that he had not seen before. It was black, and it highlighted her curves in a way that made everyone notice, including him. She had been dressing differently the last few days. She wanted Mark to notice her, and she hoped he would appreciate her.

"Is that a new outfit?" he asked. "It makes you look very beautiful."

"You flatter me," Maggie said, "and I like it. I think I'd like to visit with you tonight after I get off work if you aren't too tired."

"I would like that."

"Do you have to travel again tomorrow?" she asked.

"I don't think so," he replied. "I will be in the warehouse in the morning, but I don't plan to travel."

Mark waited in the bar for Maggie to get off work. He had one and then two and then three drinks. He was tired, so the vodka was a bit more effective than usual. As Maggie got ready to leave, Mark stepped off the barstool, and the alcohol made him feel extremely light-headed.

"C'mon. I'll walk you to the car so you can go home," Maggie said. "You look tired. You should probably get some sleep."

"No, please," Mark told her. "I need to walk, and I want to be with you."

They walked to the park, where they sat on the bench. There was a chill in the air, but the stars were beautiful, and the temperature brought their senses to life.

"Maggie, you are a great woman. Such a hard worker, honest, and so sincere," Mark said.

"You are a man who makes me feel special."

"I am going to tell you something, Maggie. I am involved in something I do not like. I don't know what to do about it, but I feel that I need to do something to make a difference for people that I have never even met before. I feel trapped between something I cannot stop and something that I must stop."

Maggie looked at Mark. "Can you tell me want you want me to do to help you?"

"It is something I must do alone," Mark said. He stopped for a moment. "I can't tell you anything about it. It is not good."

"Mark. You can trust me. You know you can."

Mark gently touched her shoulder. "You have made me realize something, Maggie. You have made me realize that I am still alive."

"You have made me realize that I want someone to be with," Maggie said. "I never really wanted a relationship, but with you, I want that."

"Maggie, you must trust me that I will do the right thing. If I went back to Chechnya and asked you to come with me, would you do it?"

Maggie was quiet.

"I know that there is Aden, and I know that he is your world. We will only be in Chechnya long enough for me to make things right with my family, and then we will go wherever you want to go in the world."

"Mark, it would be impossible for me to live without you in my life. I feel that even though we have only been together a short time. I didn't know how I would feel about us. I didn't know how it would go. I really almost hoped that it was not the way I thought it might be, but it is. I cannot fight that, but I cannot move Aden all over the world. I could wait until you make things right. I feel as though I have been waiting my whole life for you to be with me. When you return, we could meet and share our lives. I promise that I will wait for you, however long it might take."

"Maggie, you have been a whole life to me in a very short time." He kissed her softly. She pushed close to him. He hugged her, and they held on to each other.

"I will walk you home," Mark said. "Your son will be waiting for you."

"When will I see you again?"

"Soon," Mark said. "Very soon."

Mark drove back to his apartment. He knew what he had to do. He hoped he could do it swiftly and quietly.

Chapter 24
Off Script

Brian Lattis was slouching in his unmarked car outside the cheese warehouse. He watched Mark slip through the loading dock door and into the dim interior. This was the first time that they had seen him actually enter the warehouse.

There had not been much activity at the warehouse for the past couple of days.

Not much going on here, thought Lattis. *I wonder if there is another site.*

Mark walked into the warehouse, where a truck was being loaded, and he went into the office. The secretary was busily processing orders.

"Where are Nathan and Simon?" he asked.

"They've been out all week, Mark," she said. "All that I know is that they are traveling."

"Did they say when they would return?" Mark asked.

"No, I'm sorry, they did not say," she replied. "I guess you have heard the news?"

"What news?"

"We're closing the business. I have been asked to close out the sales and cancel any other orders."

"What?" Mark blurted out. "When? I mean, why did they make this decision?"

"I'm sorry, Mark. I don't know." She began to weep softly. "I don't know what I will do. I have my family to support. What will I do? Nathan and Simon made the announcement, and then they left. They said they have to travel. It was so sudden. I'm sorry. I just don't know what to do."

"I'm sorry," Mark said. "I didn't mean to snap at you." He reached in his pocket and pulled out a roll of hundred-dollar bills that he had taken from his account at the bank. He counted out ten of them and gave them to her.

"I cannot accept this," she said. "You are going to be unemployed as well, and they didn't even bother to tell you. They seemed like such nice people, and I liked them. I'm sorry that you didn't know."

Mark put the money in her hand and closed it around the money. He kissed her hand. "It is fine for you to take this," he told her. "You will do well. Good-bye."

She hugged him and turned away. "Good-bye, Mark."

Mark turned and walked out the door. *This is falling apart*, he thought.

He had not even finished his thought when he walked from the warehouse and got into the car. He did not notice Brian Lattis as he drove by his parked sedan.

Mark drove to the second warehouse quickly. Lattis had a hard time keeping up, but he was able to stay a few blocks back from Mark.

"He's moving," he told Duncan Furgeson on the cell phone, and he gave him his location.

"I think I will drive down there," Furgeson said.

Mark walked into the warehouse. It was empty. *Where is the van?* he thought.

He walked out of the warehouse and got into the car. *Well, it looks like that isn't all that is going on today*, Mark thought as he saw the two black sedans sitting down the block.

Mark had to think quickly. He got back out of the car and walked down the alley. As he rounded the corner, one of the men began to follow him. It was time to make a decision.

Chapter 25
May I See You Again?

"About last night. I—" Michael began.

"Michael, I thought it was amazing. You were so considerate of me, and I'm sorry that I led you on. It was not my intention to do that. It was, well, so easy, and I shouldn't have given in so easily," Marie said.

"Marie, what I wanted to say was that I understand completely," Michael said. "I have never felt like this with anyone. I totally understand, and all that I want to be sure is that we see each other again. Please say that you will stay with me."

"You got it, big boy." Marie laughed.

Michael laughed as well.

"I'm getting ready to go to work," Michael said. "I hope that we have an easy day."

"I hope so too."

"What are you doing today?" Michael asked.

"The station is at the police convention at McCormick Place today, and I am scheduled to interview some of the participants," Marie said. "There is someone from the FBI speaking today, and I will be interviewing her as well."

"Okay, babe. Have a great day," Michael said.

"You too, sweetie. Maybe we can see each other tomorrow. I will be in the downtown area tomorrow at the police convention again," Marie said.

"I hope so," Michael said.

"Gotta go." Marie paused. "I love you."

Michael was quiet.

"Did I say something wrong?" Marie asked.

"I love you," Michael said.

Marie was quiet.

Michael said quietly, "I've wanted to say that from the first day, from the day you first came up to me on the rig. I knew there was something about you."

"When can I see you again?" Marie asked.

"Stop by the firehouse and see me tonight," Michael said.

"I will."

Marie and Michael each had their days in front of them, so they said their good-byes and went on with their days.

Chapter 26
Confession

Brian Lattis stepped around the corner of the alley. He had seen Mark enter the warehouse, and he wanted a closer look. The area was dimly lit, and it smelled like concrete and steel.

Suddenly, he was keenly aware that someone else was there. He opened his coat to reach for the weapon, and suddenly there was a cold large handgun behind his right ear.

"If I wanted to kill you, Agent, I would have already done it. I am not a killer," Mark said.

Agent Brian Lattis had been taught how to disarm someone at the academy, but this man knew the tricks as well. If he was going to shoot, he probably would already have done it.

"All right," Lattis said. "What do you want from me, Magomed?"

"Where is the other agent? There are two cars," Mark asked.

"He is still in his car. I was going back there," Lattis answered.

"Call him and tell him to come over as well."

"How do I know that you will not kill us both?" Lattis asked.

"Turn around," Mark said. As Agent Lattis turned around, Mark took a step back and placed the gun inside his belt behind his back.

Lattis looked at Mark. He picked up his cell phone and dialed it. "Duncan. Come on over here. I think Mr. Domechian has something to tell us."

Furgeson came around the corner with his gun drawn.

"You can put the weapon away," Lattis said. "He had the chance to kill me, and he didn't. I was stupid and have worked behind a desk too long. I have no good reason to trust him, but I do."

"Something terrible is about to happen in this city," Mark said. "I am the only one who can stop it."

"How much nuclear material did you get?" Lattis asked.

Mark looked him in the eye. Obviously, these men knew most of the story already. "Not enough for fission, but enough to cause a lot of problems."

"God help us," Furgeson said.

"When?" Lattis asked.

Trial and Commitment

"I don't know that," Mark answered. "I am not in the inner circle any longer. I don't know when they will do it, but it will be soon."

"How will they do it?" Lattis asked.

"The bomb will be in a rental van. It will be detonated near the government buildings in downtown Chicago," Mark stated. "The van was in this warehouse until two days ago, and now it is gone."

"Maybe the plan will not happen," Furgeson said.

"It will happen!" Mark said. "I am surprised that I am not dead already. There was no reason for them to let me live."

"Why?" Lattis asked. "Why would they do this?"

"To make it look like the terrorists have done it. Is the chatter up on the websites of the extremist groups? It will be, and the terrorist group that will be responsible for the chatter will have nothing to do with it. The terrorists took their business away, and they want them punished for their actions."

"Why are you telling us this?" Lattis asked.

"I told you, I am no killer!" Mark said. "I want to go back to Chechnya and care for my family. No innocents should have to die for this. This is not about killing innocents."

"I cannot make any promises," Lattis stated. "I am an agent. I can't offer you anything, but perhaps I can help if and when the time comes. How do we stop them? How can we do it?"

"You can't," Mark answered. "But perhaps I can."

Chapter 27
The Firehouse Meal

Michael smiled as Marie pulled into the parking lot at the fire station. She had sent him a text saying that she was bringing dinner for the firefighters. She had rearranged her schedule at work.

"Hi!" Michael greeted Marie and smiled sweetly. "Thanks for coming. I really wanted to see you."

"My producer gave me the evening off since I finished the story that I was working on early this afternoon." She smiled and gave Michael a kiss on the cheek.

"I'll help you take the groceries in," Michael said. They took the bags into the kitchen. The firefighters usually did the cooking, but Captain Smith agreed that a new chef for the evening might be a good thing for the men.

Michael stood by the counter and looked at her. She never ceased to amaze him, all five feet seven inches of her beautiful frame. Her dark hair was perfectly trimmed just above the shoulders. He body was something that any fashion model would envy except as she had stated to him one night, "I'm not built to be a model—not proportioned correctly. Not nearly skinny enough." Michael told her that her proportions suited him just fine. He got a kiss on the cheek for that comment.

Cliff came in from the bay. "Doc, did you want me to get the grill fired up for—" He stopped in his tracks. "Well, hi, Marie! What a pleasant surprise!"

Captain Smith came out of his office and walked into the kitchen. "Hi, Marie! Thanks for offering to cook for us. Wow, look at all this food. Did Michael buy this?" He laughed.

Michael rolled his eyes. "They love me."

"Well, Captain Smith, may I use Michael to help me cook, or is fraternizing with the firefighters not allowed?" Marie asked.

Captain Smith looked at Marie. "As far as meals are concerned, fraternizing is not only allowed"—he looked at Michael and laughed—"it's an order!"

Michael washed his hands and opened the drawer to get a knife to start cleaning the chicken. The firefighters went into the bay to check on some supplies that they were restocking the jump kits with. Michael and Marie were alone. Marie stole another kiss.

"You are beautiful," Michael said. "You didn't have to do this."

"I wanted to," Marie said.

As they cut the chicken and vegetables, Michael got out another pan.

"What's that for?" Marie asked.

"I think Cassie will be here for supper if they get freed up from the hospital. She doesn't eat meat, and the guys tell her that she is on her own to pick out the meat, but I always try to be sure I cook part of the meal without meat for her."

Marie looked at Michael. "I think that's very kind of you." She was sometimes quite surprised by the things he said and did for others.

"Cassie has shown me a lot out there in the field," Michael said. "She knows a lot, and to the guys, well, she's kinda like their mom. I know that sounds silly because she is younger than most of them, but she takes care of us."

Marie smiled. "Maybe I'll do a story on her someday."

"Good luck with that!" Michael laughed.

Marie was quiet for a bit. "Michael, you told us at the bar the other night about the lady that you saved. When you saw her, what was that like?"

Michael stood quiet for a minute. "Once I realized who she was, it was like all my energy was poured out of me, and I was unable to feel anything. She was alive! I feel that it wasn't of my doing. I was there because I was supposed to be there for her."

Marie looked into his eyes. "I can't even imagine what it was like."

"It was a feeling of life—pure life and beauty and hope—and a feeling like everything was right, and I had a sense of purpose," Michael said. "Like when I look at you."

Marie looked at Michael. She smiled.

The two of them prepared dinner, and the ambulance crew was there for the meal.

DJ, Cliff, Captain Smith, Cassie, and her partner were there with Michael and Marie for dinner.

"This is really great, Marie," Cassie said. "The flavoring is really great!"

"Mom taught me how to cook," Marie said. "I don't do as much cooking as I would like to."

After dinner was over, the firefighters gathered up the dishes. Marie went to the kitchen and began to get the water ready to rinse the dishes before she put them in the dishwasher.

"Oh no, no, no, ma'am," Captain Smith said with a smile. "The rule around the firehouse is the cook cooks, and the rest do dishes."

"It's no problem," Marie stated.

Cliff came into the kitchen. "The other rule is that nobody argues with the captain." He smiled at Marie.

"Who am I to argue, then?" Marie laughed. "I do have to go, though. Gotta go back to the station to pick up something that I forgot."

Michael helped Marie carry her things to her car. "This was pretty amazing, you know," Michael told Marie.

"Michael, I—" Marie began.

Michael took his finger and gently touched Marie's lips. "Shhhh." He kissed her softly.

When they had kissed, Michael whispered in her ear, "I love you."

Marie said, "You scare the hell out of me sometimes, but I love you very much. I'll text later when things slow down. I won't be able to tomorrow; we are in the film vault looking for some material for a story."

"Film vault?" Michael asked.

"It's really a vault," Marie said. "Climate controlled and everything. It has real tape-editing equipment. It's on the third floor of the studio, kinda over the side door where I came out the first night we went on a date."

"You're the reporter," Michael said. "Don't the interns do the research?"

"I have one with me tomorrow; her name is Sydney. I continue to do most of my own research," Marie said, and she kissed Michael one last time. "Gotta go."

Michael watched her drive away. He sat on the tailboard that night, and he even said a prayer of thanks for what he had been given.

Chapter 28
The Clock is Ticking

Mark sat quietly in the office with Agents Lattis and Furgeson. He looked at his watch. Midnight. Maggie would be getting off soon.

"I have to make a phone call," Mark said.

Furgeson looked at Lattis, and Lattis nodded. "If you have gone this far with us, I will trust you to go the rest of the way."

Mark walked to the lobby and looked out the window at the night sky. The buildings of the city were brightly highlighted against the dark sky, a contrast Mark noted as he dialed his phone.

"Mark, where are you?" Maggie asked.

"I am with the FBI people in the office in Chicago."

"FBI? What's going on? Are you all right?" Maggie was confused.

Trial and Commitment

"I am all right. I have some business to attend to, and then hopefully I will be able to come and see you soon."

"I don't like this, Mark. I have a bad feeling about this."

"I made this mess," said Mark. "I have to work my way out of it."

"Mark, I want to see you again." Maggie wanted to say something to make him feel better. She sensed the fear and frustration in his voice.

"Maggie, I have made a mess of my life. I have been a bad man in many ways. I had no respect for anyone. I have just used them."

"Mark, it's all right."

"Maggie, please let me finish," Mark said. "I just want you to know that whatever happens, I had no intention of using you or hurting you. You have made me come back to life, and I am very grateful for that."

"Mark, please be careful." Maggie said. "No matter what happens, I just want to see you alive again, anytime, anywhere that I can."

"You will, Maggie—I promise you that you will. Now I have to go, but tell your son I want to take him to a baseball game and get to know him too."

"Mark, I want you to be with me," she added quietly.

"I want that too, Maggie. I want that very much, but for now, I have to go."

Mark held the cell phone against his forehead. *I don't even have a picture of her*, he thought.

He walked back into the room where the agents were on the phone.

Duncan Furgeson offered him a cup of coffee.

"Thank you," Mark said

"Why are you helping us with this? I don't understand. Why didn't you just leave the city?" Furgeson asked.

"Did you live in the UK?" Mark asked.

"I did," Furgeson said.

"And you chose to come here and work?"

"Yes," Furgeson said.

"And you have family in the UK?"

"Well, yes," Furgeson said.

"Well, what if you did something stupid that would keep you from ever seeing them again? What if they had lost their faith in you but you knew you could make things right again?" Mark asked. "How would that make you feel? I want to see my family again, and I realize I was the problem. I want to find a way to be the solution."

Furgeson handed Mark the coffee. "We'll see if we can help you to be the solution."

Brian Lattis was talking to his supervisor, Special Agent Robert Nettles. "I don't think we have that much time, sir. This could very well go down tomorrow or the day after, but it will be soon."

Mark walked over to the desk and sat down. He nodded in approval.

Nettles viewed Lattis as a good field agent, but some of his investigations had turned into wild-goose chases, and he was growing impatient.

"Brian, it's getting late, and I'm tired, so unless you can give me some compelling reason why I need to turn on these special teams now, I'm hanging up and going to bed, and we will discuss this in the morning," Nettles said.

Lattis took a deep breath. "He could have killed me. He had a gun to my head because I was stupid, and he didn't kill me! He wanted to tell us that something terrible was going to happen. That has to mean something."

There was a long pause. "What do we need? I'll be there in an hour."

"Okay. I think that I have his attention," Lattis said. "Now how do we find these people?"

Mark said, "I don't think we will have to wait long."

Chapter 29
Time to Move

"What are you doing here?" Mr. B. asked Nathan.

"Our delivery team that was to take the device into the city was arrested last night and charged with narcotics violations," Nathan answered. "I'm going with you. We have to act now. If one of the delivery boys talks, this could blow the whole thing wide open."

"And they might," Mr. B. said. "These deliverymen are gang members that use narcotics regularly. Chances are they were using some kind of drug that would make them very needy by now and ready to talk for a fix."

"What happened to Mark? Why didn't he agree to be part of this special delivery?" Mr. B. asked.

"He is off the grid. I don't know where he is. He is most likely in Europe or Canada trying to get a flight to Russia. Who knows and who cares? We got what we needed from him," Nathan said. "I'm not sure that I ever really trusted him to begin with."

Trial and Commitment

The van pulled out from an abandoned car dealership in Bolingbrook and headed toward the city.

"This thing handles like a pig," Mr. B. said. "I should have replaced the tires. Too much weight in the back."

"It only has to go a few miles," Nathan added. "Then we will put it out of its misery."

"If these damn truckers don't smash us flat before we get there," Mr. B said as another truck went around them and blew his horn.

They were reaching the intersection of I-294 and I-55.

"Aren't you going in this way?" Nathan asked.

"Accident on the inbound Eisenhower," Mr. B. said. "I'm going to Lake Shore Drive and north into the city."

"That might be jammed up," Nathan said.

"It's all jammed up," Mr. B. said. "This is Chicago, man. I would like to stop for coffee, though."

"We're going to detonate a bomb, and you are going to get coffee?"

"Yep," Mr. B. said. "All in a day's work."

They pulled off the interstate to a local coffeehouse.

"Oh, the heck with it," Nathan said. "Get me one, too, with sugar and cream. I'll buy."

"Nothing doing, boss," Mr. B. said. "This one's on me."

"You'd better take that flak vest off before you go in," Nathan said. "Might also leave the guns in the van."

Chapter 30
Moving Resources

"We have the hazardous materials team and tactical response teams located at Midway standing by, and we've contacted the Illinois State Police to see where their closest weapons of mass destruction teams are located," said Special Agent Nettles to Agents Lattis and Furgeson. There were additional agents flown in overnight at his request. "That's a lot of horsepower that somebody's going to have to pay for if this is a bust. Although, really, I sure hope it is!"

Lattis looked at one of the lead agents that had arrived. Her name was Krista Young. He knew that she was from DC. He had seen her before in training at the FBI academy. She had soft brown hair that fell to her shoulders, and she was a swimmer and liked triathlons. Krista Young was smart, beautiful, and driven to the cause that she had accepted with employment with the bureau. Lattis was pretty sure she would get the call to come to Chicago, so when Nettles told him that she was on the way, he was both happy and nervous at the same time. He knew that she was a graduate of MIT and her specialty was WMD events. He knew that she liked the job; in fact, she loved the job. Lattis also knew that senators and representatives in the halls of DC liked her and trusted her.

Lattis asked sheepishly, "Do you think we are onto something here?"

Krista Young said, "I talked to your guy Magomed over there, and either he's a hell of a liar or we've got a legitimate concern here, and I'm damned surprised that we haven't been hit yet."

Lattis breathed a sigh of relief as Nettles looked at him over his glasses.

"I talked to the guys in Springfield at STIC, and they are talking with their emergency management counterparts about State of Illinois resources if we need them," Nettles said. "Illinois has a team that can be used to work with radiation releases if we need them."

"I'd get them en route," Krista Young said. "If nothing else, we can learn about their capabilities and drink coffee." She leaned back in the chair. "We knew that this Russian or Ukrainian uranium was on the market, and it doesn't surprise me that this guy found some. His buddies, the arms dealers ... we kinda knew that they or someone like them existed in the States. There are a few shadow groups operating in the United States, and I think, from what he told us, this might be one of them. We could never get them out in the open. Most of the groups are a small organization, so they can fly under the radar. From what our guy Magomed tells us, they tried to cut a deal, or I should say that the terrorists tried to cut a deal with them and took all their guns and tried to kill one of the bosses." She paused. "The guys and gals in Indy are en route to bust the warehouse where they took the guns earlier in the week."

Lattis looked at the other three. "Mark said that everything that they had was being moved from Chicago."

"If they were closing down the warehouses and moving guns, I'd say we are on the verge of something here. I just hope we call the shots here and not them." Krista Young said. "Are you going to get something out through the JTTF on what this van looks like and who might be driving it?"

The Joint Terrorism Task Force is a locally based team of terrorism response professionals. The JTTF in the Chicago area was in full support of the bureau on such operations.

"Mark thinks maybe the drivers are some contract drug sellers that they paid to do it," Lattis said.

"I'd get the info out ASAP if I were you," Agent Young said.

"I agree," said Nettles. "Let's get out what we have through the JTTF and be especially sure that the Chicago Police Department gets it to their officers."

Chapter 31
A Random Encounter

Mr. B. entered the restaurant still fully equipped with enough weapons to take on a small militia. He noticed two men sitting at the counter with shirts that said CHATTANOOGA PD on the chest. He overheard their conversation.

Sergeant Larry Jefferson and Lieutenant Tom Cruthers were sitting at the counter sipping coffee and waiting on their breakfast. Both were from the Chattanooga Police Department in Tennessee. They were attending the police convention at McCormick Place. They were last-minute registrants, so they were forced to stay outside of the city, and most of the hotels in the city were out of government-rate hotel rooms. They stayed in Bolingbrook. They had attended that reception at McCormick Place after the previous day's session and spent time in the hospitality suite.

"I told you she could drink you under the table, Tom," Jefferson said. He laughed. "You don't get to be a commander in a big department unless you know your way around the business."

"Well, she was cute, and I think she liked me," Cruthers said.

"She liked your money!" Jefferson said. "Besides, every girl in the police business knows exactly what she is doing when she gets around us law dogs." He smiled at Cruthers, who rolled his eyes and shook his head.

"Here you go, boys," the waitress said. "Two hangover cures with eggs." She slapped Cruthers on the shoulder. "You'll be all right by at least noon and ready to go again tonight. Welcome to Chicago!"

The waitress walked over to Mr. B., who had come to the counter. "What can I get for you, Rambo?"

"Two large coffees. One black and one with cream and sugar," Mr. B. said. He glanced at the police officers sitting at the counter and quickly looked away.

Jefferson looked at Mr. B. and thought, *Is that a weapon he has in his pocket? And why would someone be wearing a bulletproof vest and tactical pants?*

Mr. B. noticed the police officer looking at him and again quickly looked away.

Jefferson looked at Mr. B. "Are you a police officer?"

"Um, yep," Mr. B. said. "Ordnance team for Cook County. Yep, we're training today."

"I'm Sergeant Jefferson, and this is Lieutenant Cruthers," Sergeant Jefferson stated. "We are here for the police convention."

"Here's your coffee, sir," the waitress told Mr. B.

Mr. B. looked at Jefferson and said, "Yes, me too. We're doing some training at the convention. Gotta go. Have a good day at the hotel." He handed the waitress a ten-dollar bill. "Keep the change, sweetie," he said, and he quickly walked out. As he went through the door, he almost spilled the coffee. He gave the officers a nervous smile and walked to the van.

"What the hell was that all about?" Cruthers said. "This is a convention for supervisory personnel, and my buddy Frank is on the Cook County bomb squad. They don't dress like that."

They watched Mr. B. get into the van and drive out of the lot. The van swayed as it pulled out of the lot and quickly sped away.

Sergeant Jefferson laid a twenty on the counter. "C'mon, Tom. There was something really weird about that, even by Chicago standards. Let's see where this guy is going." The two officers walked out of the café and headed toward their squad car that was parked in the lot near the café.

"Okay, but let me get that ibuprofen in first," Cruthers said, and they got into their unmarked squad car and pulled out onto the highway. They purposely stayed far enough behind the van not to be noticed.

Jefferson and Cruthers followed the van on the interstate. The van made some erratic moves as it made its way toward the city.

Cruthers looked at Jefferson. "I think this medication is starting to work, Larry. My head feels better. Now, if I may, just

Trial and Commitment

how do you propose we go about this? We can't stop these characters, and we are a million miles from home, and this car radio can't talk to anybody in Illinois, so just what do we do? We don't even know if these guys are just some plumbers that decided it was 'let's look like a cop day.'"

Jefferson looked at him. "Do you think the guy with the vest and the guns—and I do say *guns*, as he had a semiauto pistol under his pants on his lower leg—was just playing cop today?"

"No, I don't. That's why I agreed to this," Cruthers said.

"I've got an idea," Jefferson said. "These FBI WMD guys and gals are all pretty well connected. Let me call Agent Resnik and see if he knows somebody in Chicago that he can put me in touch with."

Cruthers looked at him. "Resnik. He's a sharp guy!"

Agent Resnik was the FBI WMD coordinator for Chattanooga and southeastern Tennessee.

Sergeant Jefferson dialed the cell phone of Agent Steve Resnick.

Resnik answered Jefferson's call. "Agent Resnick. May I help you?"

"Nick, this is Larry Jefferson. This is gonna sound like I've lost my mind, but we are following a van on … hang on a minute." Jefferson looked at Lieutenant Cruthers. "Which road are we on?"

"Interstate 55, I think."

"Interstate 55. This van is doing some pretty weird things, and the guy driving it was dressed like a military dude when he came into the coffee shop where Lieutenant Cruthers and I were eating breakfast. We just thought it was weird, and I was wondering if you knew anybody at the bureau here in Chicago that we could call."

"Let me call someone who I think might be able to help us; she just happens to be in Chicago," Resnick said.

Agent Krista Young was returning from the restroom when her cell phone buzzed. The caller ID showed that it was her friend from Chattanooga, Nicholas Resnik.

"Hi, Nick. It's Krista. What can I do for you?"

"Krista, it's always a pleasure," Resnik said. "I've got two of my local guys in Chicago at the police convention, and like most good cops, they can't leave the great state of Tennessee without mixing business and pleasure. Their story is kinda strange, and I'm going to connect them, as they need the folks in Illinois to take over for them. I know it sounds weird, but they are following a suspicious vehicle. These guys are trusted friends, so I know they aren't just giving me the business. Knowing that you are there now, I thought it might be more advantageous for you to tell me who to call up there so I can get them back to their convention duties. Can you please get a name for them?"

Krista Young knew that in police work, intuition sometimes was worth a ton of good investigative work, and if you didn't follow your instincts, you might be a good agent but not a great one. The hair on the back of her neck stood up. "What kind of vehicle, Nick?"

"I think they said it was a van, but what tipped them off was that the driver is dressed to look like a vigilante, and he's armed to the teeth."

"Nick, can you put them on with me?" Agent Young asked.

"Sure, stand by." Agent Resnik paused. The phone clicked, and the calls were merged. "Larry, I have Agent Krista Young in Chicago. She wanted to talk with you just a bit about the gentleman that you had an encounter with."

"Agent Young, this is Sergeant Jefferson of Chattanooga PD, and I have Lieutenant Cruthers with me," Jefferson stated. "Agent Young, I know that you have better things to do, but we were hoping that the locals could do a stop-and-search of this suspicious vehicle for us, as we have no jurisdictional authority here in Illinois."

"Sergeant Jefferson," Krista Young stated, "I think right now the last thing we want is for you to give up the pursuit until we can ascertain exactly where you are at so we can continue this pursuit. We are looking for a van right now that we want for a possible WMD event."

"Well, ma'am, we are following them, but I wouldn't call it a pursuit."

"I understand, and thanks," Agent Young said. "Stand by a minute."

Agent Young walked back into the conference room. She asked Agents Lattis, Furgeson, and Nettles to close the door. "I know this sounds crazy, but we have a couple of Chattanooga PD supervisors following a suspicious van on its way into the city, and if it fits the description of the van that Magomed talked about, it might be worth taking a look."

"Agent Young, there are a ton of suspicious vans in the Chicago area," Nettles said.

"I know, I get that, but let me get these guys on the speakerphone." Agent Young put her phone on the table. "Nick and Sergeant Jefferson, I'm here with Agents Furgeson and Lattis and Special Agent Nettles in the Chicago office. We are here on a credible tip of a possible WMD. Tell us about who you are following and what you are following. Give us your exact location, please."

"Well, ma'am," Jefferson said, "this guy was acting suspiciously this morning while we were having breakfast and …" The phone connection was beginning to fade.

"No, no, no," Agent Young said. "All we need is to lose this connection."

Jefferson's voice was heard again. "I think we turned going north onto Ashland Avenue. Like I said, ma'am, I don't want to be a bother."

Agent Young raised her hand to the people in the room so that everyone knew she would do the talking. "Sergeant Jefferson, please give us the exact location of where you are and the description of the van before we lose this connection. I want you to stay with this van until I call you off."

"Yes, ma'am," Jefferson said. "We are at Ashland and West Twenty-First Place, and we are going north. This is a white rental van with Speedy Rental on the side of it, and the driver was a white male, approximately fiftyish, and he is armed. This van is weaving a bit, so there will be no need to defend the stop."

Nettles picked up the phone. "Yes, Sarah I need a CPD supervisor on the phone. Not sure what district it is, but in the area of Ashland and I-55. Thanks."

"Sergeant Jefferson, please write down my number and give me yours in case we get disconnected," Agent Young stated.

It was like time dragged on forever as they exchanged cell numbers, but once each could reconnect with the other, they decided to establish a direct line.

"Nick, thanks for hooking us up," Krista Young stated.

"My pleasure, Krista," Agent Resnik said. "Hope I don't see you on the news unless it's an arrest."

"This van meets the description that Magomed gave us," Lattis stated. "I'll take Duncan, and we will be heading in that direction with Mark—I mean, Magomed."

Nettles said, "Hold on, Brian. I don't even know what we have here. I'm not ready to commit resources to this just yet."

"You know having them out there might help us maintain contact as an extra pair of eyes on the street," Agent Young said.

Nettles looked at her and then at the agents. "Go, but be damned careful. I don't like any of this."

Lattis and Furgeson left the room. As they walked by Mark, they motioned for him to come along.

Nettles talked with a CPD supervisor and gave him information on the van. The CPD supervisor told Nettles that he would have his beat officers begin looking for the van.

Agent Young asked, "Sergeant Jefferson, where are you now?"

Jefferson stated, "They just turned toward the city on Madison Street."

"This is getting really close," Krista Young said. "I don't like it. Sergeant Jefferson, you and the lieutenant need to be really careful out there. These two might be a couple of crazies that have decided that they don't like having you on their tails."

"We are in traffic near the University of Illinois at Chicago," Jefferson said. "It may be hard to keep up with them."

As the agents and Mark left the Chicago office, Lattis explained to Mark what was going on. He told him about the van and the driver.

"That doesn't make any sense," Mark said. "As far as I knew, they were going to contract the delivery of the van with some gangbangers that they were friendly with."

"Who would the guy be that they were talking about?" Furgeson asked.

"All I knew him to be was Mr. B.," Mark answered. "He built the bomb."

Lattis and Furgeson exchanged glances. Lattis felt like he had just been exposed to some horrific fact that he never wanted to acknowledge in all his duty days. This might be the real thing!

"There must have been a change of plans," Agent Lattis stated.

Agent Lattis's cell phone rang, and he answered it and listened for a moment, and then said, "Thanks, Agent Young." Turning to the others, he reported, "They just turned north toward the main part of the city."

"They want to get to LaSalle and Dearborn Streets," Mark stated.

"We have about a mile to get them stopped, then," Agent Lattis replied.

"We have more distance to cover than they do. We'll never get there in time," Agent Furgeson said.

Mark wondered if this had all been for nothing.

Chapter 32
Point of No Return

Nathan was surprised when Mr. B. pulled the van over to the sidewalk on the north side of Randolph Street. The van was at the corner of Randolph and North State Street near a pharmacy. Mr. B. handed Nathan a bag. "This is where you get out, Nathan."

"What do you mean?" Nathan asked.

"This is a second detonator in that bag. If you don't hear a boom in five minutes, hit the button, and you have three minutes to get the hell outta Dodge."

Nathan said, "I don't think you have to do this. We can get the van there together and …"

"I built this damn thing, and I'm going to see to it that it's done right—" Mr. B was cut off in midsentence as he and Nathan spotted a Chicago police cruiser traveling south on State Street stopped.

The officer got out and motioned to Mr. B. to move the van to the sidewalk and get out. The officer activated the blue lights. Nathan looked at Mr. B, who yelled, "Get the hell outta here, Nathan!" He jammed the accelerator to the floor, throwing the van forward and knocking Nathan to the sidewalk. Nathan watched as the van sped away, and he saw the van round the corner of Randolph onto North Dearborn Street. The police cruiser did not give up on the pursuit.

Sergeant Jefferson and Lieutenant Cruthers had caught up to the van and were just going to pull behind it as a police cruiser turned in front of them. "Watch out!" Jefferson shouted as Cruthers slammed on the brakes.

Nathan was watching Mr. B. speed away, with one and then two Chicago police cruisers in pursuit of the van. *This isn't what I thought would happen*, he thought.

Suddenly, Nathan felt himself being pushed against the glass of the building by a man. It was Jefferson. He and Cruthers had stopped a few cars away from the van and watched the whole chase ensue. They instinctively got out of their car and made their way toward Nathan.

Nathan let out a yell and dropped the bag with the detonator. "Leave me the hell alone!"

As the van reached the corner of Dearborn and Randolph, it impacted a police cruiser, which sent the van into a skid from which there was to be no return.

The van slid on its side, passenger-side down near the southeast corner of the Richard J. Daley Center. The van was going toward the south on the one-way street, and many cars that had just began to go toward the north as the traffic control light turned green swerved wildly to get out of the way.

Mr. B. lay dazed for a moment, but he regained his senses just enough to realize that the van was on its side. "The hell with this!" he said, and he reached between the seats. His last thought was that perhaps his former boss was watching from the window at the Daley building. He took a deep breath and pulled the trigger. He had built the bomb very well—none of his remains were ever found.

Nathan saw a fireball just one block ahead of him. The impact of the blast knocked him down and threw Sergeant Jefferson to the ground as well. They all lay dazed for a moment, and the effects of the blast wave moved over them.

Chapter 33
Effect of the Blast

The heat and blast wave of the bomb incinerated everything within half of a block of the bomb's detonation. Because the shaped charges were directed toward the passenger side of the vehicle and the vehicle was on that side, the vehicle lifted off the ground, and the explosion caused a forty-foot-deep crater to be formed in the street and in the street level below. The diameter of the crater was thirty feet as the blast tore through concrete and steel and into the openings below the street.

Anything or anyone on the Daley Plaza within the initial blast wave was destroyed or killed.

The real damage was to the buildings in the immediate area. The southeast corner of the Daley building partially collapsed as the support beams were twisted and sheared off.

Within a two-square-block area, every piece of glass that faced toward the blast and most windows that were on the sides of the buildings were either shattered or disintegrated. Even glass panes on the James R. Thompson Center, which was a block away from the blast site, were sporadically broken.

Cars within a block of the blast site on Dearborn Street were thrown like models down the street.

Fires erupted because of spilled fuel and broken windows. Many materials exposed to the heat were instantly incinerated.

The radioactive material was thrown about in many different-sized chunks and particles, embedding in concrete, steel, glass, and wood. A large amount of it would stay in the crater as the shaped charges blew it downward and then outward. The deposition of the material was not uniform, and generally it impacted structures that it could hit like a missile. There was no thermonuclear detonation, as the bomb was not intended to cause that.

The blast wave moved outward from the detonation site and was channeled by the topography of the man-made canyons that it was forced through. Buildings that the blast wave impacted were damaged, and their facades were literally stripped off and crashed to the streets below adding to the carnage.

Power, telephone, water service, and all communications in the area went down immediately.

Anyone on the streets within one block of the blast was either killed by shrapnel, burned, or rendered deaf because of the blast wave.

The wave also moved up, causing the air to be drawn through the streets as though by a giant vacuum cleaner as the fireball began to take shape and expand. The heat from the blast was so intense that it was felt for a three-square-block area. The cloud blackened the sky as it developed. The air was relatively thin because of the low humidity, so the blast wave rose quickly.

The Milwaukee–Dearborn Subway ground to a halt with major damage to the structures under the blast site.

The blast effect caused a mini-earthquake and knocked many people to their knees or to the ground.

The blast was felt for a half mile around the area on the streets and in buildings.

The only positive outcome of the detonation was that Mr. B. had mixed two barrels of ammonium nitrate fertilizer and diesel fuel together to enhance the effects of the high-order explosives. The impact caused the barrels to break open, and the materials was consumed in the blast and became part of the fireball.

Chapter 34
Too Close for Comfort

Agent Lattis was just south of the corner of West Washington and North Clark Street and was approaching the detonation site as the car was hit with the blast wave as it proceeded north. Lattis saw something out of the corner of his eye, and then the car was thrown upward violently. He was thrown into the air bag as it deployed. He noticed that Duncan was thrown forward as well. He felt intense pain in his head and shoulders, and everything went black.

Mark was the first to regain consciousness, and he realized that not only were they trapped but that there was a fire near their car. He felt a lot of pain in this right shoulder. Both agents were unconscious.

Mark tried the door handles, but the handles were jammed. He could not get out the driver's side, as another vehicle was pinned against that side of the car. He lay down in the backseat and kicked the window on the passenger side as hard as he could, and the window shattered and exploded out of the car. *Gotta get the hell out of here*, he thought.

As Mark managed to get himself out of the car, he realized that Lattis and Furgeson were still unconscious. He tried to get the front-passenger door open with no success. He managed to finally get the back-passenger door open, and he lowered the driver's seat and somehow managed to pull Agent Lattis out of the car.

A fire was near the driver's side of the car. It had started in the car next to them that had been thrown into their car. Mark lowered the seat that Duncan Furgeson was in. Furgeson had a lot of blood near his nose and mouth, and he gurgled as Mark tried to move him. *He's drowning on his own blood*, Mark thought.

With all his strength, Mark managed to pull Furgeson out of the car as well. He dragged both men to the sidewalk of the intersection of Clark and Madison Streets. He laid Duncan on his side to allow the blood to drain from his nose and mouth.

Brian Lattis was starting to wake up. Mark looked at him. "It was the bomb; you were unconscious. Furgeson has been hurt badly. Most of the people in the cars around us are dead. We were lucky!"

He gave Lattis a few moments to recover. "C'mon," Mark said. "We have to get Duncan out of here and head south out of the radiation. I know that there will be some."

"Does he have a concussion?" Lattis asked. He was still trying to regain all his senses. His head really hurt.

"I don't know," Mark said, "but he has swallowed a lot of blood. We need to move now."

The two men carried Duncan Furgeson two blocks to the south. They stopped at a McDonald's restaurant that was quickly becoming a makeshift casualty collection point.

Chapter 35
The End of a Plan

The blast knocked Jefferson, Nathan, and Lieutenant Cruthers to the ground, which allowed Nathan to break free from the men. Because of the way that the blast wave was channeled, it did not affect the area that they were in as severely as other areas around them. They had escaped the worst of the blast wave and were not seriously injured. Their location had allowed them to be shielded from the major impact of the blast wave.

Nathan thought, *I gotta get out of here.* He realized that the two men who had pushed him to the ground were some sort of law enforcement officers. He quickly reached in his belt and removed a weapon that Mr. B. had given him that morning. He aimed at Sergeant Jefferson and fired.

Sergeant Jefferson rolled away, and the bullet struck him in his left upper arm. Nathan aimed the gun at Cruthers next but realized that a gun was being aimed at him as well. He felt intense pain that he had never felt before, and suddenly everything went dark and cold.

In addition to his other duties on the department, Cruthers was a champion in Tennessee combat shooting challenges. He drew the weapon, and his instincts automatically kicked in. The "two to the body and one to the head" training technique was ingrained in his muscle memory as he pulled the trigger. Nathan never even got off a second shot at Jefferson. He died almost instantly.

"C'mon, Larry," Lieutenant Cruthers said. "We gotta get you to a hospital."

"We're in Chicago, Tom. Where are we going to find a hospital?" asked Jefferson as he grimaced from the intense pain in his arm. "Look at our car."

The sedan that they had been driving had been hit by other cars as drivers tried to stop short of the blast location. It was jammed in the middle of other cars and could not be moved.

"We'll walk till we find one," Lieutenant Cruthers said as he tied a makeshift bandage around the wound.

Both men had been so preoccupied that they had not looked toward the blast location. As they did, they were both in awe as the huge cloud kept climbing into the atmosphere.

"This will be one conference we will never forget, that's for sure," Lieutenant Cruthers said as they began their trek south. Sergeant Jefferson was able to go with Lt Cruthers as he could still walk.

Chapter 36
The Film Vault

Marie and Sydney were in the film vault looking for information on the story that Marie was preparing. Marie was sitting at a viewer looking at video from previous newscasts.

Sydney had completed her last year of journalism school and had been brought on as an intern for the station a month earlier. She and Marie had instantly become friends, and Sydney admired Marie in every way.

"Thanks for helping me, Syd," Marie said.

"This is fun," Sydney said. "I'm actually getting paid to do research."

Marie was just getting up from the viewer when she felt herself being violently thrown against the wall. She heard Sydney scream, and as Marie looked up, a large metal cabinet seemed to shift location and began to fall toward her. Marie heard something break, and suddenly her left leg was pushed violently toward the floor, and she felt a very intense pain as she saw a piece of metal tear into her leg. "No! No!" Marie screamed, and then she blacked out.

Michael, DJ, and Cliff were visiting with the oncoming crew and having coffee when they heard the explosion. It shook the firehouse and knocked some items off the wall in the kitchen. The men ran to the door and looked toward the city only to see the fireball rising. They also heard what they thought might be secondary explosions.

"Marie!" Michael whispered softly. "Oh my God!"

The on-duty crew went to get their gear and began putting it on, knowing that they would soon be responding somewhere.

"Maybe nobody down there is left alive to call in," the captain said softly.

Chapter 37
Eye in the Sky

"This is the eye in the sky for your local traffic and weather, Frank Cole reporting."

Frank Cole was the ABC traffic reporter who worked each day with pilot Richard Harvey. The station had been using the eye-in-the-sky reporter for the past year, and the viewers loved it.

The two were just finishing their daily reports, and the traffic had been surprisingly light for a rush hour.

"Great day for flying anyway." Frank looked at Harvey.

"Yeah, pretty day, really," the pilot responded.

They were flying over the I-290 expressway just about to approach the I-94 exchange when they both saw the explosion. Harvey instinctively pitched the aircraft hard to the right and tried to gain all the altitude he could, having no idea how powerful the blast would be. The aircraft was hit with part of the blast wave as it accelerated from the blast site. The blast wave moved at about the same rate as the speed of sound. Pilot Harvey instinctively brought the aircraft to a hover position and slowly began to turn around.

"What the heck was that?" Frank Cole asked. "A gas explosion or something like that?"

Having done two tours of duty in Iraq, the pilot knew that was no gas explosion.

"Gas explosions don't generate that kind of blast wave," he told Frank. "That was a bomb. Get the camera up and going, and get some video for the station. I'm going to slowly get closer, but we're going higher in case there is another one of those."

Frank Cole dialed into the newsroom on the emergency line.

"Station, this is Cole. You gotta go live with this. This is unbelievable."

"Frank, this is Grayson. What have you got?" Phil Grayson was the midday producer.

"Station, we are near where the bomb went off," Frank Cole said.

"Bomb? We thought it might have been an earthquake," the producer said.

"It's a bomb, and there is a lot of damage in the area. I'm focusing in, and I can see the hole in the ground and the devastation. It's unbelievable," Frank Cole answered.

"I'll give you ten minutes, Frank, and then we gotta put this ship on the ground. I'm not sure if anything was damaged. This is a civilian ship. They aren't built to take the pounding the military aircraft are. That blast wave his us pretty good," Harvey said.

"Okay, got it. Station, let's go. Can you get the feed? Station, you gotta get the feed and make it live," Frank Cole said.

"Stand by, Frank. We are having some difficulty with the antennas and getting the signal," the producer said. "Okay, we got it. Wow! Okay, here we go. Live in three ... two ... one ... live."

"Ladies and gentlemen, we interrupt our regularly scheduled programming to give you a special eye-in-the-sky look at what appears to be a bomb in the city of Chicago." The morning anchors were still in the building and were hastily called to the set, and within ten minutes, everyone in America and three other continents that had access to television or the Internet would see it too.

Chapter 38
A Major Event

The blast was felt throughout the loop area of downtown Chicago, and there was a surprising silence of all communications immediately after the blast occurred. It took a few minutes before the 911 lines began to be filled with callers who claimed that everything from a bomb to an earthquake to an enemy attack had occurred.

The 911 communications center at the Chicago office of Emergency Management & Communications was alive with calls. The director of the OEMC was Shannon Gentry. Director Gentry knew that something had just happened that would define the course of the next few days if not weeks of response, so she did what most Americans do when something happens: she turned on the television. In fact, she turned on six televisions that covered all the local news channels plus two cable news networks. She gasped when she turned on the local ABC affiliate and saw the footage that was being shot by Frank Cole and Richard Harvey.

Shannon notified her communications director and staffed the Emergency Operations Center for Chicago.

Trial and Commitment

Shannon then picked up the phone and dialed the director of the Illinois Emergency Management Agency, the state's lead agency in disaster and emergency coordination.

"This is Julia Dietrich," answered the office assistant of the director of the Illinois Emergency Management Agency in Springfield. The Illinois Emergency Management Agency—or IEMA—is the agency tasked with managing emergency response throughout the state of Illinois.

"Julia, this is Shannon Gentry. I need to speak to the director."

There was a pause, and then the director came on the line. "This is Gary, Shannon—what can I do for you?" Gary Morehouse was the director of the Illinois Emergency Management Agency. He knew Shannon, as they had both served in the Illinois National Guard.

"Gary, I'm not sure if you know what we just had, but I'm guessing some sort of bomb was planted on-site near the government buildings on Dearborn Street. We are going to full activation," Shannon said.

Director Morehouse responded, "We just saw the live feed, and I am calling in the agencies. I'm asking the chief of operations to begin mobilizing his staff to head north if you need them. Our regional representative will be with you in the emergency operations center."

"Gary, I haven't talked to the fire commissioner or the mayor yet, but I think we need a state declaration from the governor now, and you'd probably better ask the Illinois National Guard to turn on their air assets as well."

"I'll call the governor as soon as we get off the phone, and the adjutant general will be my next call. The Illinois Department of Public Health will start getting bed availability for the area so if you have to start moving patients, you can," Director Morehouse said.

"I just hope that there are enough alive down there to move. Thanks, Gary, and I'll be in touch for a conference call as soon as we get everybody in here and organized," Shannon said, and she hung up the phone.

Chapter 39
The Response Begins

The engine and truck located at 419 South Wells Street was the first unit to arrive at the scene. Captain Geraldo Jeffers took command of the scene from the area just south of the Chase Tower on Dearborn Street. He reported heavy damage in the area and that there were multiple casualties, injuries, and fires located near the Richard J. Daley Center. He began to activate multiple box alarms, which are predetermined resource requests that bring additional resources to the scene. The amount of resources that were being requested made it a history-making day in the Chicago Fire Department.

"Stage them at the fire academy until command calls them in," Captain Jeffers told the dispatcher. "We need the incident management team to be called in as well. This is going to be a long-term operation."

Captain Jeffers was talking with one of the men on the scene when his engineer called him over to the engine. "Captain, remember when we got these a couple of years ago, and they ended up in the glove boxes? Well, just to be sure, I got it out and turned it on, and it is registering that we have some sort of radiation on-site." The engineer was holding a small radiation-detection instrument that the department had been issued a few years earlier. The devices had been in the rigs and were to be activated at any scene where there was a question of a terrorism threat.

What the engineer did not realize was that a chunk of the uranium had fractured during the blast and had embedded itself near where they had parked the apparatus. This chunk was setting off the detectors. It was a matter of dumb luck that the radiation was near the apparatus.

Captain Jeffers looked at his cell phone as he tried to call the battalion chief. The signal had been lost again. The signal was intermittent at best. "I'm going over here and see if I can call the battalion chief and let him know that we have radiation. Issue an order to all companies to begin monitoring for radiation."

"Do you want to hold the rigs and the ambulances back?" the engineer asked.

Captain Jeffers looked at the device. It was still alarming. "Yes," he said. "Hold them at the academy till we can get some accurate readings of the amount of radiation that we are dealing with."

Chapter 40
Trapped

"Marie! Marie! Can you hear me?" Sydney was gently touching Marie's arm.

She had moved the boxes and equipment off her friend after she had dug herself out of the pile of videotapes, boxes, shelving, and dust. She noticed that Marie was covered with the same debris but that she wasn't moving. Sydney could see that Marie was breathing, but she was unconscious.

Marie began to move her arm, and she opened her eyes. "Sydney, what the heck happened?"

Sydney replied, "I don't know, but the whole room came down on us."

Marie tried to move and winced in pain. Her leg was trapped, and the pain was excruciating.

Sydney moved some more of the debris, and she saw a piece of one of the shelving units stuck into and through Marie's lower leg.

"It's bleeding," Sydney said as she began to cry.

"Look, Syd," Marie said, "you are all we both have right now if we want to get out of here in one piece. You gotta be strong."

"I know," Sydney said as she wiped her tears. "I'm so scared right now."

"Okay, honey, I know," Marie said as she touched Sydney's arm. "Right now, we gotta find something to wrap my leg and stop the bleeding so I don't bleed to death in here."

"Okay," Sydney said, and she began to look around the room. She climbed over some of the collapsed bookcases to get to the door, only to find out that it was jammed. She looked over in the corner and saw some of the rags that had been used to cover the viewing equipment. She took them over to Marie, and the two of them managed to get the rags over the leg and stop the bleeding.

"Syd, that's great work. You are a star," Marie said, and she managed a smile through the pain. "Take my cell phone and get as close to the door as you can. Maybe you will get a signal."

Sydney took the cell phone. It read, "Michael, we're in the vault. My leg has a piece of metal in it. We can't get out. Please help us if you can, and remember, whatever happens, I love you." She wiped more tears and made it to the door.

"No signal, Marie," Sydney said.

"Just stay there for a few minutes; the service is probably really bad, but just keep moving the phone and see what happens."

Marie was hoping for a miracle. The pain in her leg was almost unbearable.

"Nothing, nothing. Wait a minute. I have a bar. Now two!"

"Hit Send and stay there," Marie said. The bar moved across the screen and stayed near the right side of the phone for a few seconds, but then nothing.

"It didn't go through," Sydney said.

"Copy and paste the message and try it again."

Sydney tried again and again and again and again. And finally, the message sent.

"Yes!" Sydney said.

"Oh, thank you. Thank you," Marie whispered. "Now, Syd, I need some pain medicine, so start digging through your bag that you brought in with you, and look in my coat pocket."

They found two acetaminophen tablets and an aspirin and two pills for cramps and bloating. "Please, Syd, give me the two acetaminophen tablets. That's a start."

Marie managed to swallow the two acetaminophen tablets. She shifted her weight slightly, and some of the pain subsided. Marie was able to think rationally for the time being. "That's better. Thanks."

Sydney said, "I sure hope Michael gets the message."

"He will," Marie said. She began to think about the first time they met.

"What makes you so sure, Marie?"

"Michael's strong and shy and kind and tough, and he completes me. He walked into my life that day when I was covering the fire. I know you aren't supposed to approach the firefighters at the scene, but I watched him rescue the lady. He helped the paramedics and looked so young and innocent but yet so strong and smart that I just had to talk to him. I don't regret it at all. I think—no, I *know* I fell in love that day."

"Have you made love to him?"

"No," Marie said. "I was kinda hoping that we could build our relationship first." She was quiet for a minute. "In fact, I was really hoping maybe we could wait until we got married."

Sydney leaned over and kissed her friend gently on the forehead. "I knew you were different. You really are my hero, Marie. He'll come for us. I know he will."

Chapter 41
Into the Fire

Michael, DJ, Cliff, and Captain Smith went with the on-duty crew to the fire academy. The official recall had not gone out, but since they had stayed over after the shift, they went to the fire academy with the rest of the firefighters. Captain Smith was immediately detailed to the incident command team that was assembling the plan to respond to the incident.

"This is killing me, the not knowing," Michael told Cliff.

"She's okay, man. She's smart," Cliff replied.

"If I could just talk to her!" Michael said.

"Phones are all screwed up down there," DJ said. "One of the guys here said he finally managed to text his wife."

Suddenly, Michael's phone buzzed. He grabbed it out of the holster so fast that he almost threw it. The text was from his mother: PLEASE, MICHAEL, BE CAREFUL.

"C'mon, Marie. Talk to me," Michael said quietly.

"What are we waiting on? Let's get going!" Cliff stated.

Captain Smith walked over to his crew. "One of the rigs is picking up radiation near the site. The bosses want to be sure that we don't walk into something we all regret."

One of the firefighters from the on-duty crew was standing by Michael. "Maybe it was a nuke," he stated.

"It wasn't a true nuke—at least it wasn't a nuclear detonation; I can tell you that." The men looked over and saw a tall, thin young man looking at them. He was wearing a polo shirt with the letters IEMA on it. He walked over and shook hands with the men. "I'm Tom Gibson. I'm with the nuclear safety division at IEMA, and I'm on the radiological team. It wasn't a nuke, or your cell phones and radios wouldn't work. Nukes put out something called an electromagnetic pulse; it screws up communications for quite a distance. My best guess with the radiation being detected is that this was a dirty bomb. They put nuclear material in the bomb itself, and it was scattered in the blast."

"What are you doing here?" Cliff asked.

"I was here doing some calibration at the academy, and, well, I'm not leaving now. I just found out my guys in Springfield are loading up to head this way now."

Just then, Michael's phone buzzed again. It was Marie's phone.

"She's hurt!" Michael showed the phone to Cliff. "And she's bleeding!"

Michael began to collect his gear and started toward the door.

"Hold on, Michael!" Captain Smith said. "Where are you going?"

"Captain Smith, Marie's hurt pretty badly, and I'm going even if I have to walk," Michael said.

"Now hold on, son," Captain Smith said just as Cliff and DJ walked up with their gear as well.

Captain Smith and Michael made eye contact, and Captain Smith looked at the floor. "All right, all right, damn it! Go!"

Michael looked back at Cliff and DJ. "I'll go, guys. It'll be all right."

"Yes, we'll be fine," Cliff said.

"I'm sure I could use the help," Michael said.

"What about the radiation?" DJ asked. "Can we get in and get out and still be okay?"

"You can with air packs and turnout gear, and I'll help you find the areas where it is safe to go in," Tom said. "The main dangers are alpha and beta particles if they are in the air. You gotta wear supplied air when you get in there. I have no idea what they used for the source of the radiation. It could be spent fuel, processed fuel, medical waste ... who knows? You gotta get in there and sample it to see what radioactive source was used to build the device."

"Now just how are you going to get in there, Mr. Tom? You don't have any gear," Captain Smith said to Tom.

"No, Captain, but you do! This is the fire academy. Just give me a set of turnout gear and an SCBA," Tom said. "I've trained my whole career for this day! I can help them. Please, Captain ..."

"I kinda like this guy," Cliff said. "He's growing on me real fast."

"Can you wear an SCBA? Have you been trained?" DJ asked.

"I am on the state's radiological response team," Tom said.

Captain Smith looked at him intently and raised his right eyebrow.

"I can wear an SCBA; I have been trained." Tom looked down.

"All right, and boy, am I gonna get written up for this. Get Mr. Tom here some gear and an SCBA, and you guys are gonna take the reserve engine and put some spare bottles on it and some extra tools on it as well."

Michael grabbed forcible entry tools and headed for the engine. He knew his team was behind him.

Tom went to his truck and brought instruments to measure radiation. The instrument that he brought to the engine was one of the

Trial and Commitment

most modern instruments on the commercial market, state of the art in every respect. He could detect all types of radiation with it and measure the levels as well. Tom took it out of the case and attached the pan probe to it to measure the radiation that they might find on the ground or near the building. He also got two new portable detectors to put on the dash of the truck, and he also brought some pencil dosimeters that each firefighter put in the interior pockets of the coats. "These will tell us how much of a dose of radiation we each receive," he told the firefighters.

"Will I glow?" Cliff asked, smiling. He wanted Michael to relax, and Cliff knew that he could always make him laugh.

"That's not funny," Captain Smith said.

Michael shook his head and smiled. "Cliff, Cliff, Cliff."

Captain Smith had to stay at the academy, as he was part of the planning section for the response. "Get the hell in and out," Captain Smith said. "No hero stuff. Hear me?"

"Yes, sir," they all replied.

Just before they departed, Cliff went into the bay and took a battery-powered extrication tool and cutter and an extra battery for each. He put them in the rear compartment of the engine. "Never know when these might come in handy," he said.

Michael kept trying to text Marie: WE'RE COMING. HANG IN THERE. I LOVE YOU.

Unable to send, unable to send, unable to send. "Damn it!" Michael said under his breath.

They left the academy and made their way north on Jefferson Street, as the interstate was jammed as people tried to exit the city. They made their way to Harrison Street and turned east. They could see smoke rising from the site. Full suppression efforts were not yet under way, but engines and trucks were beginning to be positioned to begin the attack on the fires.

The engine went north on State Street and stopped at the corner of State and Washington Streets just to the east of the television station where Marie and Sydney were located.

The firefighters donned their SCBA equipment, and Cliff and Michael grabbed the rescue tools and the irons and began walking toward the television station. Tom turned on the radiation instrument, and it began to chirp softly.

Just before Michael put the facepiece on, he sent one last text.

"Still trying to reach her?" DJ asked.

"No. I'm sending this one to an angel of mercy," Michael said.

DJ looked at him with a confused expression on his face.

"It'll be okay, DJ." Michael slapped DJ on the back. "Thanks for coming in with me."

The men walked from the corner of North State and East Washington toward the studio. Tom noticed that the amount of radiation that the instrument was picking up began to increase. The uranium had definitely been shot out from the bomb, but the levels were not causing Tom to be overly concerned.

They found a revolving door and a walk-in door on the south side of the building where the studio was located. They were on the street level. The doors were blocked, and there were people sitting on the floor inside the lobby.

Michael had been walking quickly toward the building. He was in the lead all the way to the structure. The others quickened their pace to keep up. Michal remembered the accident on the interstate and how the lady was going into shock. That might be Marie right at that instant. They didn't have a minute to lose.

Chapter 42
Coordinated Response

Agent Young and Special Agent Nettles showed their badges to the guard at the desk of the Chicago office of Emergency Management & Communications. The emergency operations center—or EOC—had been activated to support response efforts in the city.

Shannon Gentry was on the phone when the agents walked in, and she motioned to them to come over to the table where she was. Tom Gathers, the fire commissioner, came over as well.

"I'll be back in touch with you in just a minute," Shannon Gentry said. "Special Agent Nettles, obviously you know more than we do about the fissionable material, and the fire units on scene are picking up some radioactive material. What can you tell us?"

"First of all, Shannon, this is Agent Young from our WMD DC bureau, and she actually talked to the man who knew about the bomb."

Trial and Commitment

The fire commissioner looked angrily at the agents. "You had a guy talking to you? How long ago did you know about this? Why didn't we get an initial heads-up?"

"Let's get one thing really clear here, Commissioner," Krista Young said. "We shared everything we had as soon as we verified it through the JTTF. CPD went out with this today. We think the radioactive material is Russian or Ukrainian fissionable material; the high-order explosives that were used to propel that radioactive material are anyone's guess. We aren't really sure what they bought. They had several kilograms, and it was packed with the explosives in the vehicle. Our DC folks are looking at some models now based on the quantity and the size of the blast hole, but one thing we know is the blast did disperse the materials. How far and how much deposited in the area, we don't know yet."

"Relax, folks," Shannon Gentry said. "We're all on the same team here, and here is a problem that we have to deal with. The walking wounded are already in Rush, Mercy Medical on Dearborn, and Stroger hospitals, and they have detected radioactive material there. These hospitals are on bypass. What we have to do is get the decontamination teams in place so that we don't contaminate any more hospitals. We have three main collections of walking wounded. They are at the James R. Thompson Center, Grant Park, and at a McDonald's just south of the blast site, so we need to decon people before they leave the sites, and we need to get hazardous material response teams to these hospitals around the city now so that we don't lose any more ERs."

When a hospital is on bypass, the hospital emergency department does not take patients because they are overwhelmed or because there is a circumstance that does not allow them to receive additional patients. The hospitals went on bypass because of the contamination.

"All right, Shannon, I get it," the fire commissioner said. "We will get engine companies to the hospitals with special operations guys who know about decon, and I also had the deputy commissioner call Red Center and tell them we needed all the MABAS level-A HAZMAT teams that they could muster and get them on the way. I also ordered Illinois Task Force 1 for search and rescue in the Daley building and around the area. We are also requesting some of the special teams from MABAS that can do search and rescue."

"What about ambulances?" Shannon asked.

"We've pulled a special alarm box for ambulances," the commissioner said. "We should have an additional forty to fifty in the hour, and I have a special box pulled on engines and trucks as well. We have ladder towers and straight ladder trucks en route for fire suppression."

Red Center is the Mutual Aid Box Alarm System (MABAS) dispatch center located in Northbrook, Illinois. The MABAS system has many specialized teams throughout Illinois that can do specialized response functions, such as search and rescue, hazardous materials response, and other functions. Task Force 1 is the Illinois version of a FEMA search-and-rescue team. They can search for and rescue trapped victims. The team was created in response to the 9/11 attacks and was created to be used for major collapses in the state.

A man walked up to the group and said to Shannon, "Ms. Gentry, the Illinois Radiological Task Force is departing Springfield within the hour. They shanghaied two C-130s from Peoria to get them here. I just found out one of their guys is on-site with a CFD engine near the blast site." He held up his hand. "Now before you even ask, he self-deployed with the CFD guys. Nobody told him to go in."

The gentleman speaking was Harold Smith. He was the regional representative from the Illinois Emergency Management Agency. It was his job to come to the EOC when it was activated.

"Well, I don't care why or how he got there. What I do want to know is, what is he seeing on the ground?" Shannon asked. "Is he able to tell how much radiation is really there?"

Harold stated, "He says it's there, but he is not getting a lot of it. The radiation is not evenly dispersed. Cell phone communication is spotty. He is talking to his folks back in Springfield."

"Our HAZMAT guys and gals are going to Midway," Special Agent Nettles said. "Maybe we can hook up with these guys from Springfield near the site and get a better picture of what is going on."

"I can make that happen if you'd like," Harold said. "I'll see if Springfield can get the Illinois National Guard folks involved so that they can get them where they need to go. There are some Illinois National Guard units at Midway and in North Riverside that we may be able to tap into for help."

Shannon looked at Harold. "Go for it, and tell them thanks."

"Will do," Harold said, and he went back to the desk.

"Has the mayor declared this a disaster yet?" Commissioner Gathers asked.

"He will when he gets here," Shannon answered.

The mayor of Chicago has the authority to declare an area a disaster if he so chooses. That gives his response agencies the ability to do their jobs without worrying about whom is paying the bill. It also allows the mayor to have special powers to manage the event.

"This radiation is a big deal," Shannon said. "We need to get a handle on this fast before the public finds out about it and starts to panic."

Chapter 43
Moving out of the City

"We need to get him going now. Did he ever regain consciousness?" Cassie asked as she did a quick assessment of Agent Furgeson. "He's FBI, correct?"

"Yes," Brian Lattis said.

"You're not looking so well yourself," Cassie said to Lattis.

"I'll be all right," Lattis answered. "Most of my headache has gone away, and things aren't so fuzzy."

Mark looked on as Cassie assessed Furgeson.

"I will go with him and make sure he is well taken care of," Mark said to Lattis and Cassie.

"He's going to Edward Hospital in Naperville when we get him going. It might be a long ride," the treating paramedic told Mark.

"I assure you, I don't have anywhere to go," Mark told the paramedic.

"Who got him here?" Cassie asked.

Agent Lattis and Mark looked at each other.

"Well, you saved his life," Cassie said. "We gotta get him going. His blood pressure is kinda high. Not sure what is going on with him."

Lattis looked at Mark. "I'll leave you with him. I'm going to get to headquarters somehow and get them the info on what has happened. I trust you with him. You pulled us from the car, and I know that you will help him through this mess we are all in."

"I failed," Mark said. "This is my fault."

Brian Lattis looked at Mark. "As Duncan is fond of saying, 'Failure is a relative thing, mate.' Keep me posted when you get where your cell will work."

"Okay, let's get his clothes off and get him going," the paramedic said to Mark.

It is not the policy of CFD or any of the private ambulance service companies to transport any family members or friends with patients to the hospital, but protocol was not something that was being taken very seriously right at the moment.

Mark was walking with the paramedics as they took Agent Furgeson to the ambulance. He looked at the people at the restaurant as they passed. Mark's eyes met the eyes of the people, and all he saw were distant stares. He said to the paramedic, "This is how those people must have looked in the lifeboats when the *Titanic* sank. They are distant; they have no hope."

The paramedic looked at Mark. "They are the faces of death. They have all put on their death masks—either their deaths or the deaths of the people around them."

Mark caught sight of a young woman looking intently at her smartphone. It was black, but she kept staring it as though she had lost her whole world. For the first time since it all began, Mark felt great remorse. He fought back tears.

Duncan Furgeson was placed in the ambulance, and Mark sat in the front seat on the passenger side. He looked back as the paramedic was placing an IV in Duncan's arm.

"I think your buddy has a pretty good chance once we get him to the hospital," the driver said to Mark.

Mark picked up his smartphone to send a text to Maggie. He had completely forgotten to send something to her in all the action. *She must be beside herself,* he thought. It was a simple text: I'M ALL RIGHT.

CHAPTER 44
Rescue

Tom looked at the firefighters. "No detectable radiation in here. You can take off the SCBAs."

Michael walked to the front of the building. This was where the studio had been. No one had been broadcasting at the time of the blast, but two of the staff had been working near the studio and had walked to the front of the building to see what was going on when the blast occurred. Their bodies—or what was left of their bodies—lay in a tangled mass of steel, glass, and wires in the studio. Michael had to swallow hard before he could continue. There was no way that they were getting to the upper floors from here.

As he walked back into the lobby, he saw that Cliff and Tom were talking to the people there—employees of the station who had sought shelter in the enclosed sections of the building as the blast happened. These people couldn't understand Cliff and Tom, as their hearing had been affected by the passing blast wave. They managed to tell the people to leave the building and walk to the east, where they could get away from the carnage. Tom was convinced if they went immediately to the east that they could avoid any permanent damage to their skin and internal organs from the radiation. They fashioned covers for their noses and mouths from some cloth towels that they found in the nearby restrooms. Cliff had done a quick assessment of the building and determined that there was a stairway that would get them to the third floor.

The stairway was inside a concrete silo that made its way to the upper floors. There was surprisingly little damage to the walls, but there was still some debris in the stairway that they had to clear as they made their way up the two flights of stairs to the third floor. Michael was in the lead the whole time.

As Michael managed to pry open the door to the third floor, they entered a long hallway that was covered with remnants from the ceiling tiles that had collapsed.

"Marie!" Michael yelled at the top of his lungs. "Marie, let me know if you hear me!"

Marie had been resting on Sydney's leg. They had talked for a while longer, but Marie was becoming quiet. Marie had taken the rest of the medication, and her ability to fight off the excruciating pain was waning.

"This pain is almost too much, Syd," Marie whispered. "I can't take this much longer."

The metal piece that had gone into Marie's lower leg was a jagged section of a shelf vertical support that had been ripped from one of the shelves as it fell over. It was a direct hit on Marie's lower leg and had shattered her fibula as it hit. That had been over thirty minutes ago. Marie's body was out of adrenaline, and she was slowly going into decompensated shock. Her circulatory system was on the verge of collapse. Sydney had never let go of Marie's hand the whole time that she was sitting with her. Sydney was about out of energy herself. The tears flowed freely down her cheeks.

"Marie!"

Sydney heard it. They were in the hallway.

"Michael!" Sydney yelled as loud as she could. "Michael, we are in here!"

"Here!" Michael stopped by the heavy door that was the entrance to the film vault. "They are in here! Cliff, bring the spreader!"

The spreader is a tool with two arms that open in a Y configuration. It is used to pry open anything that is shut and refuses to open. It is hydraulically operated and can generate an amazing amount of force.

Cliff inserted the spreader between the doorjamb and the door. The door strained a bit and then opened easily.

Michael was the first one in the door. What he saw caused him to gasp. Marie and Sydney were near the back of the room, and they were lying in a pile of debris. There was a large piece of metal in Marie's leg.

Michael gently crawled back to where they were. He held Marie tightly in his arms. "We'll get you out of here." Michael was fighting back tears as well as he could.

Marie looked at Michael. She felt a surge of energy and managed a smile. "Okay, then, get me out."

Michael and Cliff surveyed the piece of metal that had sliced into Marie's leg. "We are going to have to secure it above and below the leg," Cliff said to Michael.

"I'll secure it as well as I can," Michael said.

Tom removed some of the debris so that he could help. "I'll help secure the metal piece with you, Michael." Their eyes met, and Michael knew he was working with a professional.

"We gotta hold this this perfectly still while I cut it," Cliff said. "We can't move the piece around in her leg and open up any bleeding."

Michael, DJ, and Tom each grabbed the metal piece above Marie's leg and did their best to stabilize if as Cliff began the cut.

Marie grimaced as the pain increased, but she did her best not to cry out.

Cliff made the cut cleanly about six inches above Marie's leg, and they found that the piece was not attached near the floor, so the first cut freed the leg and the metal.

"We gotta find something to put her on to carry her out," Michael said.

"Wait a minute," DJ said, and he walked over to the side of the room and took out his knife from the pocket of his turnout gear.

He fashioned a long leg splint from some cardboard and even cut out the indentation for the shrapnel. They fashioned the makeshift splint to Marie's leg using some packing tape that they found in the corner of the room, fastening it securely.

"That does feel a little better," Marie said.

They began the slow process of the move out of the building. Sydney held Marie's head as the firefighters and Tom maneuvered her torso and legs through the hallway and down the stairs. Marie only moaned in pain a couple of times. Each time, Michael said, "I'm sorry."

"It's not your fault, guys," Marie said. "At least we are moving."

They made their way to the lobby, and they laid Marie on a couple of chairs.

"Now I guess we wait till we get somebody here," DJ stated.

"We don't have a lot of time," Cliff replied.

Michael walked to the door and opened it. "My angel's here," he said and smiled.

Cassie and one of the private ambulance company crews were near the door. They had parked a block away and were just making their way to the building.

Cassie went over to Marie, bent down, and hugged her. "I couldn't let my boys down," she said. She did a quick assessment of

Marie's vital signs and looked intently at the firefighters. "We gotta go, though. Marie isn't looking so good right now."

Michael stopped in his tracks, and the thought that he had not allowed to enter his brain hit him and took almost total control of his feelings. *You could still lose her. She is going into shock.* Michael froze. His thoughts went to the first time that she had looked him in the eyes at the fire scene. He had been so shocked to look up and see those big, dark eyes and her beautiful face. It had totally reset his whole life, and he couldn't bear to lose her.

"Hey, big boy, you gonna help us here?" It was Cassie, and they were ready to go to the ambulance.

"Oh, sure. Sorry, Cas," Michael replied.

They made their way to the ambulance. They gingerly loaded Marie into the back of the ambulance. Michael took off his turnout gear and left it at the scene in case there was any radiation on the gear.

"Good luck," said Cliff. "We'll see ya real soon. DJ and I and "Edward Teller" (he was referring to Tom), are going to see what the radiation levels are around the building so Tom can report those to his team. Then we're going back to the academy to get reassigned."

"I can't thank you guys enough." Michael stopped suddenly as he saw Sydney by the door. "Guys, I gotta say something to her."

Michael and Sydney looked at each other. Michael hugged her tightly. "Thanks. Syd. You're a hero!"

"She loves you, Michael. She wants to spend the rest of her life with you. Please take care of her," Sydney said, and she left to rejoin the others.

DJ was helping Sydney to the nearest casualty collection point so they could check her out to see if she had sustained any injuries.

"Where are we going?" the driver asked Cassie.

"We gotta go out of the city," Cassie said.

Michael looked at Cassie. "We're going to Rush."

"Rush is on bypass, Michael," Cassie said.

"Because of the radiation," Michael said. "I talked with Tom, who was with us. He works for IEMA's radiological response division, and there isn't that much radiation. Besides, Dad's working today, and maybe I can get her into the OR quicker."

"Okay, Michael. Your call," Cassie said.

Michael took Marie's hand and gently cleaned her forehead with a washcloth that the ambulance people had given to him.

Cassie and the paramedic were desperately trying to establish an IV in Marie's right arm. They had decided to try to find a vein in the antecubital fossa, on the inside of the elbow. The veins were larger and more accessible. They managed to get the catheter in the vein, and they immediately began to infuse some life-saving fluids.

"Marie, I can't give you any morphine till we get your blood pressure up a bit," Cassie stated.

"I know, Cassie. I can't believe this. The pain is just so bad," Marie said.

"I know, Marie, and as soon as we get some fluid in, I'll give you some morphine," Cassie said.

The drive to the Rush University Medical Center emergency department was slow, and the traffic was heavy even though the police were attempting to get the cars out of the area.

Once they arrived, they were taken back by the number of people that were still coming to the ER.

"So much for bypass," the driver said.

As they took out the stretcher and moved toward the ER door, Marie looked at Michael. "Once we get in, if you have to leave to go and help some of the other people, I understand."

"Not a chance. He's here to stay," Cassie said. "We can do without him, at least for now." She slapped Michael on the back.

The trauma nurse who was attempting to triage the patients as they came into the emergency department looked at the crew. "Guys, we are on bypass. What's the deal?"

Michael looked at her. "I need to talk to Dr. Fortenier as soon as I can."

"He's in surgery, I'm sure. Now look, let's get this lady to a bed, and I'll do a quick assessment," the nurse said.

Michael walked toward the elevator. "I don't have time for this."

The nurse walked toward Michael, and as she was about to stop him, Cassie touched her arm and walked her back. "That's Dr. Fortenier's son," she told the nurse. "I think with any luck this may be his daughter-in-law someday."

"That's Michael?" the nurse said. "Why didn't you tell me? Let's get her over here on one of our beds."

"She needs another IV," Cassie said. "I didn't get to give her any morphine yet. This girl has been through a lot today."

"Okay, I'll get a nurse to help you. It's been a day here as well. How bad is it down there?"

"Bad," Cassie answered, and she took the IV start kit from the nurse and began looking for a vein on Marie's other arm.

"I never thought I'd be a pincushion, Cassie," Marie said. She managed a painful smile.

Michael made his way up to the third floor. As the elevator door opened, he saw his father at the desk with a nurse, talking about a case.

"Michael, what are you doing here?" his father asked. He seemed confused to see his son standing before him. "Where are your shoes?"

Michael realized that he had not had any shoes on since he'd left his turnout gear at the scene.

"Dad, Marie has been hurt. She has a piece of metal stuck in her leg, and she's shocky. Cassie got an IV in, but she's not doing well. I need some help." He stopped speaking as his voice cracked.

"Michael, we're pretty shorthanded here right now," his father said.

"I didn't know where else to go," Michael said. "Please just at least look at her."

"Where is she now?"

"In ER now with Cassie and a nurse," Michael said.

"Okay, let's get her up here," his father said.

Chapter 45
National Implications

Agent Young and Special Agent Nettles were in a room away from the EOC. Krista Young had received information from headquarters to find an area where they could make a secure call.

Stanley Reynolds had been the director of the FBI for about a year. He had worked diligently to make the organization professional and forward thinking and he relied heavily on staff members who were intelligent, candid, and resourceful. He liked Agent Krista Young.

"Krista, this is Stanley, and I have General McKinney from the Joint Chiefs here with me. Are you sure this is a secure line?" Director Reynolds asked.

"As far as I know, it is, sir," Krista Young said. "I have Special Agent Nettles here with me as well."

"Okay, I'll get right to the point," Director Reynolds said. "The president will need to address this situation. He has been in

Trial and Commitment

contact with the mayor of Chicago, but I need to know from you exactly what intel you have on this, Krista. Can you tell me if any of the known terror groups are involved in this?"

Krista Young explained what she had obtained from Mark and Agents Lattis and Furgeson as she tried to gather all the information that she could.

"So as far as you know, there is no influence of any terrorist organization or external government in this?" Director Reynolds asked.

"No, sir, not that I know of."

There was silence on the line.

"I can't say that there is absolutely no outside influence by any terrorist organization," Krista Young said.

"So this bunch of home-growns acting without our knowledge or the knowledge of any law enforcement agency out there in the Chicago area pulled off one of the deadliest attacks in our country's history, and we didn't know anything about it beforehand other than this guy who decided to turn himself in and cooperate?" Director Reynolds asked.

"That is what I have been able to ascertain by talking with the people here."

"Where is this guy now?"

Krista Young looked at Nettles. "He was with two of our agents trying to stop this attack, and we haven't heard from them since the blast."

"So you don't know where he is?"

"No, sir, I do not know," Krista Young answered.

"You know, this would have been a hell of a lot easier for the president and the American people to swallow if you had told me that this was a known terrorist organization or some fragmented foreign government."

"I understand that completely, sir."

"Krista. Go find this guy and the agents, and let me know when you have found out about their status. And, Krista, when you find this guy, tell the Chicago agents he is ours to arrest and detain, and I want him alive! In the meantime, share everything you know with Special Agent Knowles here at headquarters so that we can start working the intel on our end as well."

"Yes, sir, will do," Krista Young replied.

"And, Krista, remember, if we have someone to show the world that we have in custody, that will go a long way to secure our credibility and make the next group that tries this think twice."

"Yes, sir."

They hung up the phone.

"We gotta find Lattis and Furgeson fast, and hopefully Mark is still with them." Nettles looked at Krista.

Krista Young said, "What happened to our two officers from Tennessee that were following the van?"

"Guess we go looking for them as well," Nettles said. "I have some agents that I trust implicitly, and I'll get them in here and have them begin looking for Lattis and Furgeson and the Tennessee officers. It's not like Lattis and Furgeson to not let us know what they are up to. Something must have happened to their communications capability."

"I just hope that they weren't too close," Krista Young said.

Chapter 46
Edward Hospital

The ambulance that was transporting Duncan Furgeson arrived at Edward Hospital in Naperville, Illinois. The hospital had been designated as one of the trauma facilities for ambulance transport outside of the Chicago area. There were hospitals from Milwaukee to Kankakee receiving patients from the scene once they were triaged at the casualty collection points.

As the stretcher was removed from the ambulance, the nurse looked at Mark. "Are you a family member? We need some information, please."

Mark looked at the nurse intently.

"Well, are you a family member, or aren't you, sir?" the nurse said. "We need some information on this man."

"He is Agent Duncan Furgeson," Mark said. "He is with the Federal Bureau of Investigation. I am a ... well, a friend."

"All right, sir. Why don't you go to the registration desk while we do a quick assessment and see what we have here, and we'll get to you really soon. What happened to him?"

"We almost drove into the blast wave," Mark said. "The windshield imploded, and he was hit with it. He was bleeding and choking on his blood."

"Was he able to get out of the car on his own?" the nurse asked.

"No. I pulled him out," Mark said. He and the nurse made eye contact, and she looked directly at him.

"Did he ever regain consciousness? Do you know what I mean by that?"

"He never regained consciousness. I have been with him the whole time." Mark looked intently at the nurse.

The nurse saw the pain in Mark's eyes and reached out and touched Mark's arm. "I will see to it that we get him in quickly. Thank you for what you did for him." The nurse looked at the attendant charting the information. "This one will need a complete workup of the head and cranial area as soon as possible. He never regained consciousness."

Within a few minutes, Duncan Furgeson was on his way for a scan of his head and neck.

Mark went with the team as far as the waiting room and sat down. He looked intently at the door. On the other side of the door was freedom. He thought of his father and Aysa and … Maggie. *Maggie!* He pulled the phone from his pocket. The battery was at 25 percent. *Better make this fast before it dies.*

He texted:

MAGGIE, I HAD A LOT OF CHOICES TO MAKE TODAY, AND IN MANY CASES, I MADE THE WRONG CHOICES, BUT HOPEFULLY IN AT LEAST ONE OF THOSE CHOICES I MADE THE CORRECT ONE. I WATCHED PEOPLE DIE TODAY IN PART BECAUSE OF MY STUPIDITY, BUT I ALSO WATCHED PEOPLE LIVE, AND I INTEND TO LIVE, AND I HOPE TO SEE YOU SOON.

Chapter 47
Mercy Medical

Sergeant Larry Jefferson and Lieutenant Tom Cruthers made their way south to Mercy Medical at Dearborn Station. The hospital was surrounded by many patients that had walked to the location from the blast area. Sergeant Jefferson was feeling the effects of the bullet wound, and he was experiencing a lot of pain.

The nurse came out to them. "We are triaging patients, and then you will be sent to another hospital. Do you think that you are contaminated from any radiation that the bomb emitted?"

"Radiation?" Lieutenant Cruthers asked. "What do you mean? It was a dirty bomb?"

"Yes, that is exactly what I mean," the nurse said. "Do you think you were contaminated?"

"No. I don't think so," Lieutenant Cruthers answered. "We were at least a city block away."

"Well, we still need to get you looked at to see if you have any radioactive materials on your clothing. What's the problem with this man? May I see the injury?"

"He was shot," Lieutenant Cruthers said. "We are police officers. We were following the van. It's a long story."

The nurse looked at Lieutenant Cruthers with disbelief as she looked at Sergeant Jefferson's arm. "Come over here and get a blood pressure for me, would you, please?" she said to another person who was assisting her.

The attendant came over and took Sergeant Jefferson's blood pressure. "How long have you been bleeding?" she asked.

"Thirty minutes or so," Sergeant Jefferson said. "I thought we had the blood flow stopped."

"Please come with me," the nurse said as she took Sergeant Jefferson to the emergency room door. "We need an IV in this man quickly, and some morphine," she said to the technician at the door.

The whole emergency room was full of patients. Some were on the beds, and others were on stretchers that had been brought in and placed in the hallways. There were patients with cuts, bruises, possible broken bones, and any injury that could be written about, talked about, or even imagined within the hospital walls.

For the most part, the patients looked like they had been attended to in some fashion. Lieutenant Cruthers could see down a long hallway through a door that was opened. Near the end of the hallway, he saw the unmistakable sign of bodies that had been covered with blankets. Not everyone that had been brought here was going home tonight.

Lieutenant Cruthers's phone chirped. He looked at the number and read his text. THIS IS AGENT KRISTA YOUNG. PLEASE CONTACT ME. I'M SORRY THAT I HAVE NOT MADE CONTACT SOONER.

Lieutenant Cruthers texted Agent Young and told her where they were and what had happened.

The text came back: WHERE EXACTLY ARE YOU? WE ARE SENDING ONE OF OUR AGENTS TO GET YOU.

"Hey, Larry! FBI is coming for us! Guess they want to talk to you!" Lieutenant Cruthers smiled.

Lieutenant Cruthers was talking to Sergeant Jefferson and texting Agent Young at the same time. A PERPETRATOR WAS KILLED IN A SHOOT-OUT. BODY IS IN FRONT OF A WALGREENS ABOUT A BLOCK FROM THE BLAST SITE.

Agent Young texted: MUCH APPRECIATED, LIEUTENANT CRUTHERS. SEE YOU SOON.

The IV was established and flowing, and some morphine had been administered. Sergeant Jefferson looked a whole lot better than when they had arrived.

Within twenty minutes, there was an agent at the door of the room where Sergeant Jefferson and Lieutenant Cruthers were sitting. Sergeant Jefferson was in a seated position with the IV still in his arm.

A doctor appeared at the door. "Under normal circumstances, this man wouldn't be going anywhere, but if you promise me that you will keep a close eye on him, I'll let him go. We bandaged the arm up pretty well, so there shouldn't be any more bleeding, and we have administered one thousand CCs of the IV fluid and some antibiotics in case there was any contamination from the bullet. I'd say that he looks perfused, and his color is back. But like I said, this has been anything but normal today. Take some of these pain medications with you in case the pain returns." He handed the men a bottle of pain medications.

The officers went with the agent to his car, and they drove to the FBI office building.

Chapter 48
Surgery

Michael saw Marie as she was being taken to one of the operating rooms. There were fresh dressings on her leg, but these dressings looked like they had been soaked in blood. Marie looked tired as Michael watched her as the gurney passed them by.

Michael's father walked out to where Michael and Cassie were standing. "She's lucky in one respect, as the artery wasn't cut by the metal piece, but I don't know where the metal is in relationship to the artery, and I won't know till we get in there. If the artery is nicked, cut, or torn and we open it up, it's anyone's guess as to what we can save. I have no vascular surgeon here with me today; it's me, and that's about it. I do have some really great surgical assistants."

Michael looked at his father. He hung his head.

"Go on in and see her before we start. She asked about you," Michael's father said to him.

Michael walked into the operating room. Cassie watched Michael go into the operating room.

"He busted his ass to save her," Cassie said to Michael's father. "In fact, he has busted his ass to save a lot of people in his short career. If you have ever had a reason to be proud of him, today is the day."

Michael's father responded, "There hasn't been a day that has gone by, Cassie, that I haven't wanted to tell him that I am proud of him. I always wonder about him on his duty days, and I have them marked on my calendar. I wonder about what he is doing. Were there any fires? How was he fitting in? The girl he saved from the house fire works here at the hospital. She told me what he did for her. His mother has ridden me pretty hard to tell him, but you know how it is."

Cassie touched his arm. "Tell him."

"Thanks, Cassie," Michael's father said.

Michael touched Marie's hand, and she reached out to him. "My hero," she said.

Michael welled up with tears. "You are everything to me. My life is complete with you. I want to grow old with you." He stopped and wiped a tear with his duty shirt, which left a mark of soot and dirt on his cheek.

"It'll be okay, Michael," Marie said.

"You are strong, and this is just another battle to win, Marie. I love you." He held her and kissed her.

Trial and Commitment

Michael hated the piece of metal that was stuck in Marie's leg. He didn't know quite how to relate to the fact that he hated an inanimate object. It was just some stupid piece of metal that someone had fabricated years before and had not even given it a second thought. Just a stupid, unfeeling, nonliving chunk of metal that right now meant the difference between life and death or life and loss of a limb. A piece of nothing that had turned into everything. Michael held Marie's hand tightly and kissed her forehead. "This will be fine. I know it will. You are strong!"

"Mr. Michael. You know the drill," a nurse said. "We'll come and get you as soon as we are done."

Michael held Marie's hand till they started for the door, and he gently let go.

Michael and his father passed as Michael went toward the waiting room.

"Get some coffee, Michael, and relax for a bit. I'll come and get you as soon as we are done."

Michael looked at his father. "She is my world, Dad. Everything, everything. Just please keep her alive, even if the leg.." Michael stopped short of what he wanted to say and wiped a tear with his shirt. It had already been a long day.

"I know, Michael, and we'll take care of her, I promise." Michael and his father hugged each other for the first time in many months.

Cassie was waiting for Michael as he walked out. "Michael, I gotta go. They will wonder where I got off to."

"Cas, you have no idea how much this has meant to me," Michael said.

"Michael, do you remember the car accident on the interstate?" Cassie asked.

"Sure I do."

"The lady pulled through, and the foot was surgically reattached," Cassie continued. "Not many people understand what you have to do to work together and get a job done under those conditions. I asked for you and Cliff to be with me in that car. No matter what happened, no matter how bad it got, I needed someone to be there with me to help save that lady's life. I asked for you, Michael. Get it?" Cassie was looking into Michael's eyes.

"You really are amazing, Cassie!" Michael replied.

"This girl means a lot to all of us, Michael." Cassie pointed at the OR door. "And so do you. Now get some coffee, and that's an order, Michael." She kissed his forehead and turned to go. "I'm outta here, back to the hell."

Cassie walked out the door and was gone. Michael found a coffeepot and poured a cup of coffee. He sat in the chair and looked at the OR door. Strangely, it looked like the doors to one of the rooms at Brother Rice High School. It looked like the door to the chapel. Michael sipped the coffee, and before he could finish the cup, he leaned his head back, and time slipped away.

Chapter 49
Redemption

Agent Brian Lattis made his way back to the FBI office on Roosevelt Road.

When he walked into the office, the employees looked at him as if they were seeing a ghost.

"Where have you been?" one of the agents asked him.

"Everywhere and nowhere really," Agent Lattis answered.

"Where's Furgeson and the other guy, the terrorist?" the agent asked him.

"Duncan is in Naperville in a hospital. He was almost killed when the blast went off. We are lucky to be alive. I have no idea why we are still alive. We shouldn't be. Mark, eh, Magomed is with him. Where are Nettles and Agent Young?" Lattis asked.

"They are in the OEMC at the EOC," the agent said. "They wanted to know if we heard from you. They wanted you to call them."

Lattis took out his cell phone. It was cracked and dead. "So much for military-grade durability," he said.

One of the other officers said, "Brian, you look like you have been run over by a truck. You're a mess, and you have a bruise on your forehead. Are you sure you are all right?"

"I would like some strong coffee," Lattis said, "and I need the secure line. I want to talk to Nettles."

Once he had cleaned up a bit and the office staff made a fresh pot of coffee, Lattis felt as though he might actually be getting back to his normal self.

The line was secured, and Special Agent Nettles answered the phone. "Brian, where were you? We thought you were dead. Where are Duncan and Magomed?"

"I'm going to Naperville to check on Duncan and get to Magomed. I want to get to him first, before some other crazy hothead gets out there and turns this into a shoot-to-kill situation. I would have just stayed with them, but I knew I needed to get back here and let people know what had happened. Mark pulled us out of that car after we almost got too close to the blast, or we'd both be dead now, and given the chance, he would have tried to stop that whole thing from happening."

"Brian," Nettles said, "you have an hour, and then I am going to have to turn this over to the special agents that are here from DC. This will be out of our hands really soon. The director is determined to have someone in custody for this. He wants his DC staff to arrest

Magomed, and they will handle the process from there. And by the way, I'm glad that you are alive."

"I'll be alive after a nice hot shower and a brandy," Lattis said. "I do appreciate your concern, sir; I know that I have been wrong on some things in the past."

"Well, you sure weren't wrong on this one! What do you think about Duncan?" Nettles asked. "Do you think he'll make it through?"

"I'll let you know as soon as I find out," Lattis said.

Lattis hung up the phone and walked over to Agent Sandra Macintyre's desk. She was looking through some court documents on Magomed.

"C'mon, Sandy. Come with me," Lattis said.

Agent Sandy Macintyre was a relatively new hire. She had been an investigator in a local police department and had been in the FBI for less than a year.

"Where are we going, Brian?" Macintyre asked.

Brian Lattis looked at her. "To see a friend and to hopefully save a life."

They headed to the parking lot and left in an unmarked sedan.

Chapter 50
A Life Saved

Duncan Furgeson was in surgery soon after they arrived at the hospital. The brain scan showed that there was a hemorrhage between his brain and skull, and the blood had to be evacuated quickly or he would die.

Mark sat in the lobby. An attendant allowed him to use a cell phone charger that she had brought to work with her.

He called Maggie to talk with her before the agents arrived, and he knew they would be coming soon.

"Maggie, I will be back in jail. I know that I will be, and I accept that. I am not running away from this. I was drawn into a group of people that used me to get what they wanted. They were really no different from the drug dealers, just more sophisticated and cunning," Mark said.

"As long as you are alive, Mark, that's all that matters to me. You don't know how much our long talks meant to me. The talks

Trial and Commitment

brought me out of a deep, dark valley. I know that inside, you are a good person," Maggie said.

"It's not right for you to give up a bright future to be with me and live in my pain," Mark said.

"Tell me what happened today. No, tell me what happened from the beginning of this odyssey, Mark. I want to know," Maggie said.

Mark told her about Nathan and Simon and Mr. B. He told her about the trip to see his father and about Aysa, and he told her about the bomb and how he had pulled the agents out of the car.

"Mark, you saved the agents. That has to mean something," Maggie said. "The bomb would have been built with or without you."

"Maggie, I don't know what will happen to me," Mark said. "If you will let me talk with you and be your friend, that will be everything to me."

"I would like that very much," Maggie said. While he was still speaking, one of the nurses came up to him. Time had slipped by, and Mark realized that it had been over an hour since the surgery began.

"The surgery was successful," the nurse said. "Once the anesthesia wears off, we will be moving him to a room. You can see him then if you would like to. Would you like some food? We have some in the cafeteria."

Mark realized that he had not eaten anything in quite a while, and that seemed to be the best thing to do while he waited for the rest of his life.

"Maggie, I will call you soon," Mark said, and he headed to the cafeteria.

Chapter 51
Success

Michael was sitting over in the seat with his head resting on his shoulder.

His father looked at him, and for one swift second, he saw his son sitting on the living room couch resting on his shoulder. The little boy who would fight sleep until it overcame him like a flood—the young man so tired after football practice that he frequently missed supper as he came in and fell asleep on the couch and who was now a young firefighter and a young man who had found something in his life that he desperately wanted to hold on to.

"Michael," his father said.

Michael opened his eyes. He was dreaming about walking at the bomb site with Marie and the firefighters desperately searching for …

"Dad!" Michael took a deep breath and opened his eyes fully. "Marie! How's Marie?"

"We got the metal out. It fractured her fibula in two places, and it was lying against an artery, but we got it out, and we cleaned the inside of the muscle as best we could without opening any severe bleeds. She will need some strong antibiotics for a while and probably at least another surgery to repair the bone damage. She's going to be hurting for quite a while, but I'm pretty sure we saved the leg. Her distal pulses are good, and the lower extremity pinked up pretty well, so we know the blood flow is good. She is a strong young lady," Michael's father said.

Michael hugged his father for what seemed like an eternity. They both sat down in the chairs. "This has been so surreal, like a dream, yet so horrible. There were people in her building that went to the window to see what was going on when the bomb went off. Their bodies were unrecognizable. How many people died down there today? I just can't imagine."

"We have had many, many patients here even with the threat of radiation," his father said.

"We had a technician from the state with us," Michael said. "He took readings down by Marie's building and said that it wasn't as bad as he thought it might be but that the radioactive material was thrown from the bomb like little missiles, and it is embedded in whatever it touched. But he wasn't panicky, and he seemed like a sensible guy."

"Michael, you know when you became a firefighter, my biggest fear was that you wouldn't know what it was like to work with a real bunch of professionals like I do here. I felt like the paramedics and firefighters were … well …" His father stopped for a moment.

"Not true professionals?" Michael asked.

"I guess so. I felt like they didn't know how to really care about each other, how to give of themselves freely for others," Michael's father said as he looked intently at Michael.

"They do, Dad," Michael said. "They care about me, and they care about Marie, and they have accepted us as part of their family. They helped me today to go and get her against assigned protocol. They may be written up for it. I doubt it, but they could be for disobeying a direct order. Marie wasn't our assignment. We ended up helping several other people, and we got some really good information about the radioactive materials, so I think we may be overlooked."

"I think a lot will be overlooked today," Michael's father said. "It is a day Chicago will never forget. Sad, really, that we can't save more people."

"I'm sure you and the staff did what you could for them," Michael said. "Thanks for helping Marie."

He hugged his father again, and his father went back to the OR.

A nurse came out a few minutes later. "Michael, give us a few more minutes, and you can see her. She will still be out of it; she's on some pretty strong medications, and I'm sure she's exhausted."

Chapter 52
End of the Duty Day

Nathan's body was placed in a body bag after the agents had taken pictures of the location and the body. Lieutenant Cruthers had left no doubt as to the cause of death as he had placed three rounds from his nine-millimeter Beretta squarely in the head and torso.

Since Nathan had no idea of the turn of events that were to take place, his cell phone contained all the contacts to the organization that he had been a part of. The FBI agent at the scene quickly took possession of Nathan's cell phone.

"We'll take the body to the Cook County morgue and be sure it's tagged as not to be released without permission of the Federal Bureau of Investigation," the agent said.

Sergeant Jefferson and Lieutenant Cruthers were with the agents as they secured the body.

"So what's next for us?" Cruthers asked.

Trial and Commitment

"If you'll come down to the office with me so that we can debrief and get statements, as far as I'm concerned, you two will be on your way," the agent said.

"Well, sir, being 'on our way' is a relative term," Jefferson said. "That is our car." He pointed to the blue sedan that had been wedged in a collection of cars near the curb.

"We'll have to work on that too," the agent said.

"'We,' hopefully, would be you folks in this case, as the reality of the situation is that we have a supervisor that is not going to be too happy to know that one of his newer vehicles is unserviceable, if you know what I mean," Cruthers stated.

"I'm sure that we can work something out," the agent stated. "Agent Young will be the point of contact on this one."

They drove to headquarters, and the men were taken into the office of one of the agents.

Cruthers looked at Jefferson. "Larry, I don't know about you, but I'm starving. Is there a snack machine near here?"

The agent showed him to a break area, and before long, Cruthers and Jefferson were feasting on two Snickers bars and washing them down with freshly brewed machine-generated coffee.

"You Chicagoans really know how to eat," Jefferson told the agent. "Who needs deep-dish pizza when you can have a candy bar and coffee?"

"Sorry, guys," the agent said. "It's been kinda hectic around here today, and we had a couple of agents near the blast when it happened. We're still looking into the condition of one of them."

"Sorry to hear that," Jefferson said. "It was unreal how much fire and smoke it generated."

The agent dialed the secure line at the EOC.

"Agent Young. May I help you?" Krista Young answered the phone.

"Agent Young, this is Agent Adams here at the office. I have Jefferson and Cruthers with me, and I thought you said that you wanted to talk with them when we located them."

"I sure do. You boys have had a busy day. Thanks for what you did today," Agent Young said.

"I'm not sure what we did for you, ma'am," Jefferson said. "They still got the bomb off, and that is terrible."

"It is bad, and I'm not making light of that, but there was one terrorist that isn't going to perpetrate any other acts of mischief, and your quick actions took care of that for us," Krista Young said.

"Well, ma'am, we would appreciate a call to our supervisor, as our car is definitely out of service," Cruthers said.

"I can do that, gentlemen," KristaYoung said. "Just share what you can with Agent Adams, and then we'll get you transported where you need to go or get you a rental, and we'll keep in touch. My suspicion is that there are more of these characters around the country that we will be going after really soon."

Jefferson and Cruthers both prepared written and oral statements for the agents, and after that was done, they were taken to a rental car agency and secured transportation back to their hotel, where they could rest for a bit before returning to Chattanooga, where their lives would never quite be the same.

Chapter 53
Time to Bargain

Agents Lattis and Macintyre walked into Edward Hospital in Naperville and went to the front desk to inquire as to the location of Agent Furgeson. The steady stream of ambulances had subsided, and the people arriving were family members desperately searching for loved ones.

As they approached the desk, the attendant asked, "May I help you?" It was obvious to Lattis that she had long since exceeded the work hours that she had planned on putting in for the day.

Agent Lattis showed her his badge and said, "I'm looking for Duncan Furgeson."

The attendant looked at her screen. "Were you there today?" she asked.

"I was there," Lattis said. "A lot closer than I should have been."

"How bad was it?" the attendant asked. "I can't imagine."

"It was the closest thing to hell on earth that I could have ever imagined," Lattis said.

"Mr. Furgeson is in ICU, bed 6," the attendant said. "Thanks for sharing that. I mean, I'm not looking for all the details, but it does make me realize that we are doing something beneficial here. It has been a long day."

"I'm sure that you have done your part in the grand scheme of things," Lattis told the attendant. "Thank you."

They walked up the stairs to the ICU, and just before they exited the door, Agent Macintyre looked at Lattis. "You think Magomed is here?"

"He will be, and I'll handle that," Lattis stated. "That is why *you* are here with me."

As they walked into the room after passing the central core of the ICU, they saw Duncan Furgeson sitting in bed. His head was bandaged, and his left eye was covered, but he was awake and looked at them when they entered the room.

Mark was sitting in a chair by the window, looking out at the sky and the surroundings near the hospital. He looked over at them as they entered the room.

"It is going as well as can be expected," Mark said. "I didn't know he had a daughter, but he told me to call her on his behalf, and I did. She is coming here from the East Coast this evening to be with him."

Furgeson motioned for Lattis to come over. His speech was somewhat garbled, and he could not project well. "He told me everything that happened, Brian. All of it. I can't believe that we are alive."

Brian Lattis took Furgeson's hand. "We shouldn't be, Duncan. We shouldn't be. He saved our lives when we would have been killed when the flames reached our car."

"The doctor said that he drained some blood that was putting pressure on his brain," Mark said. "He should be okay, but he will have to regain his functions. It will take time."

"He has all the time he needs," Lattis said.

Lattis looked at Agent Macintyre. "Please stay with Duncan. Mark and I are going to get a cup of coffee. We'll be back in a few minutes."

"I will," Agent Macintyre stated. She and Agent Furgeson had worked together on some cases, and she liked him. She sat by the bedside and took his hand in hers and held it tenderly. "You sure know how to add excitement to all our days, Duncan."

Furgeson managed a smile.

Mark and Lattis went to the cafeteria. There were not a lot of people in the cafeteria. There were some people eating, and some were actually lying in the booths napping.

"These people have had a rough day," Lattis said. He looked at Mark. "Duncan and I owe our lives to you, and we appreciate it. I know that you would have stopped the bomber if you could have, and I know that you have come to understand the totality of all this,

Trial and Commitment

so here is the deal. If you walk out that door to the hallway and I never see you again, well, so be it. I'll think of something. If you stay, they will arrest you, and it will go to the DC folks to work on the prosecution. I won't have much to say, but there is another option."

"What do you mean?" Mark said. "I did the unthinkable. I worked with these people, and I got the nuclear material."

"But you didn't tell Agent Young everything you told us. Correct?"

"Yes," Mark said. "You know everything."

"No, no, I don't. In fact, I don't know anything except that you wanted to stop the bomber."

Mark looked at Lattis. He had the feeling that he was being asked to do what he did best. Perhaps this time it was for his very life. "You want me to bargain with them?"

"That's what you're best at," Lattis said. "Turn state's evidence and tell what you know about what happened, but you don't know everything. For all you know, the people you worked with are still alive. How will they know the whole story, unless *you* tell them?"

"I never thought I'd be sitting with an FBI agent being told what to do to save my life," Mark said.

"Now, before we get up from here and I take you back to headquarters, I want to know everything about your family," Lattis said.

"I don't understand."

"You can't go and find them, but we can. Duncan and I can do the research in a perfectly legal way as a follow-up to the investigation," Lattis said.

Mark told Agent Lattis everything about his family. He told him about his father and Aysa and about the last meeting with his father. He listed names and places and the people that he had contacted to find his father. "It was easy for me, because they knew I was operating under the radar, so to speak," Mark said.

"It wasn't under the radar of the Russian Foreign Intelligence Service. At least not totally under the radar," Lattis said. "Russian intelligence had the guy you met with in their sights. I'm surprised that they sold you the uranium before they got nabbed."

Mark shook his head. "Imagine that. It wasn't so covert after all."

Mark stood up and shook hands with Lattis. They both went back to Furgeson's room. He and Agent Macintyre were conversing.

"Mark and I are going to headquarters," Lattis said. "Time to get Mark back before the headhunters come looking."

Mark walked over to Duncan Furgeson's bedside. Duncan held up his hand, and Mark took it.

Mark leaned down, and Furgeson said, "Thanks. Thanks for giving me a chance."

Mark gently squeezed Furgeson's hand, and he and Lattis left the room and went to the car.

Once they were en route to the office, Agent Lattis dialed the secure line at the EOC again.

"This is Agent Young. How may I help you?"

"It's Lattis. Furgeson is alive and doing well, and Mark and I are en route to the office. He agrees to turn state's evidence in the presence of his attorney."

There was silence on the line. "I don't understand," Agent Young said.

"He surrendered to me, and I will arrest him when we get to the office," Lattis said.

"Brian, this is Nettles. I think we should let the DC folks handle this." Special Agent Nettles had joined the conversation on the speakerphone.

"No, sir," Lattis said. "I will arrest him according to our protocol. The crime occurred here, and I will make the arrest."

"Okay, Lattis," Agent Young said. "He's all yours. This may really play into your future career choices."

"I'm aware of that, ma'am, but I don't plan on going anywhere," Agent Lattis said.

He and Mark drove to headquarters, and the booking of Magomed Domechian occurred at 4:20 p.m. in the presence of a state-appointed public defense attorney.

Chapter 54
The Report

Tom Gibson, DJ, and Cliff changed the air bottles in the SCBAs and began doing some exploring near the blast site. The amount of radiation that they detected was higher closer to the crater.

After a few minutes of exploring and taking readings, DJ looked at Tom and Cliff. "Time to go," he said.

They dropped all their gear near the engine by the side of the building and made their way back to the academy. Tom was furiously writing down numbers that he had obtained from the radiation detection device so that he could share his findings with the team when they arrived.

As they pulled across the street from the fire academy, they noticed several vehicles with FBI on the sides. "Hey, I know who those guys are," Tom said. "That's the FBI HAZMAT team; we did some training with them last year."

Once the engine was parked, Tom opened the door and stepped out. "I'm going to go talk to those guys, but first give me the TLDs [thermoluminescent dosimeters] that I gave you guys. We will analyze how much radiation we all got, and that way we can know if there will be any follow-up medical monitoring needed."

Tom looked at DJ and Cliff. "That was a great thing that you guys did for Michael and Marie. You firefighters are top notch with me."

DJ and Cliff smiled, and they each shook Tom's hand.

"Just please let me know if I need to microwave my breakfast from now on or if I can just cover it with my hands to get the same effect," Cliff said.

Tom smiled and headed toward the FBI HAZMAT team vans. "I'll see you guys again," he said.

Captain Smith was in the conference room on the first floor of the fire academy. DJ and Cliff stood in the hallway as he came out. "How's Marie? Where's Michael? What did you guys find down there? Did anyone get hurt?"

"Hold on, Chief." Cliff smiled. "Marie is in the hospital. Michael is with her. Tom is sharing some readings that he got from the radiation instruments with the FBI guys, nobody got hurt, and there's not even a scratch on the reserve engine."

Captain Smith smiled briefly and then looked intently at the men. "What's the real story? How bad is it at the site?"

"It's pretty bad, Captain," DJ said. "Lots of folks died there today, but my guess is that the fire suppression efforts are going well, and the radiation isn't as bad as Tom thought it might be."

"And Marie?" Captain Smith said. "How is she doing?"

"She lost a lot of blood," DJ said. "A chunk of metal was in her leg, and it was pretty nasty. She was kinda shocky. They got some fluids in her, and somehow Michael had Cassie there with a private ambulance crew. They headed for Rush. I think she will be okay, but it's going to be a long road for her to get back on her feet again."

"What about Michael?" Captain Smith said. "How is he doing?"

"He's a tough kid, Captain," Cliff said. "This will be tough on him. They have something real between them. I kinda figured that out at the academy on media day, and I was skeptical at first, but it's real, and I think that will help both of them."

"Let's hope so," Captain Smith said. "Head on down to the cafeteria and get some coffee. If you're up to it, we could use some relief on the suppression companies. We are going in on four-hour shifts."

"What about Michael?" DJ asked. "I know that there was a general recall of firefighters."

"I'll cover Michael," Captain Smith said. "I'll cover Michael."

Chapter 55
Recovery

Michael's first thought when he saw Marie was one of shock. She was lying in bed with two large-bore IVs in her arms, and she looked very pale.

Marie was still coming off the anesthesia, so she wasn't fully cognizant of her surroundings. She looked at Michael and managed a smile.

"Just relax," Michael said. "You've had a rough day."

"I'm really lucky," Marie said. "It all seems like a bad dream."

"You're safe now, and that's all that matters," Michael said.

Marie looked at him. She was still sleepy.

"I'm not going anywhere," Michael told Marie. "So just relax, and I'll be right here."

Marie drifted off into sleep. Michael held her hand. He stayed at her bedside for the next two days. The nurses made sure he was able to get cleaned up, and Michael's mother brought him clothes.

Perhaps the most frustrating thing that Michael observed was how Marie reacted to the medication. She was uncomfortable, and this was not something Michael liked.

Marie was totally bedridden. She was not able to get up and go as she pleased. Her leg was elevated so that the blood could flow freely from her leg back to her body.

On the second day after the blast, Marie's parents arrived at the hospital, having driven to Chicago from their home in Texas. Michael had never met them before. They certainly didn't fit the mold of what Michael had expected. Marie's father was of Irish descent, and her mother was originally from Mexico City, so they were the epitome of contrast. Michael didn't know what to expect when they arrived from Brownsville, Texas.

Marie's mother embraced her daughter, and Marie's father walked directly to Michael and took his hand firmly. "My daughter is alive because of you!" He hugged Michael.

Marie's mother was in tears, but she also came over and hugged Michael.

Marie had begun to improve. There was hardly any fever, and she was tolerating the antibiotics much better after the doctors had given her some medicine to calm her digestive system down a bit.

They sat and talked about what had happened, and Marie told them how Michael and his friends had come to help her in the film vault.

"So how long have you been a firefighter?" Marie's father asked Michael.

"Almost six months now." Michael responded.

"You will be the best one ever!" Marie's father said.

Marie was having some pain, so the nurse administered some pain medicine, and a short time later, Marie was asleep.

"She doesn't do so well with the medicine," Michael said.

"She never has," her mother replied.

Marie's mother and father walked with Michael to the cafeteria.

"You must be hungry," Michael said to them. "Let me buy you something to eat."

They sat down, and when they had finished eating, Marie's father spoke up. "We knew that Marie was seeing you. We also knew that she was quite happy. She has been very blessed since she came to Chicago. We were trying very hard to convince her to move back to Texas to be closer to us. She had some bad times in Nashville. She met some very bad people."

Michael looked at them and said, "I have fallen in love with your daughter. I cannot deny that."

"You have won her heart," Marie's mother said. "A mother's intuition tells me that you may become more than friends someday."

Michael smiled. "I'd like that."

Marie's father looked at Michael. "Marriage is for life. Look at us. Everyone said, 'What are you thinking? You are so different.' That has been the best part, and when Marie came along, we knew that she was the best of both of us. Irish temper and strongheaded like her mother!"

They all laughed.

"We will stay and help you for as long as you need for us to," Marie's father said. "I'm sure you may have to go back to work."

"I think that I should," Michael said. "The department has covered my shift today, but I should go and see if they need help tomorrow."

"Have they caught the people who did this?" Marie's father asked.

Michael looked at him. "You know, sir, to be honest, I haven't even paid attention to the news!"

Chapter 56
The Arraignment

Mark did not care for the Metropolitan Correctional Center, Chicago. He was held in a cell in the solitary confinement unit. The cell was small, and the guards were very militaristic in their approach to everything. Mark was held at the facility and was not allowed any visitors.

He was allowed to talk with Maggie on two occasions, and she told him that she would come to see him as soon as it was allowed. Mark tried again to convince her that she should not worry about him and should look to move on with her life. Maggie would not have anything to do with the conversation. It was that thought that kept Mark motivated to make it through each day.

Mark was interviewed by agents and a representative from the United States Attorney's Office for the Northern District of Illinois. Mark did exactly what Agent Lattis had advised. The conversations had been lengthy, and each time the attorney left, Mark was told that they would consider his situation. The court-appointed attorney was with Mark on each occasion and advised Mark what he could say without jeopardizing his ability to plea-bargain his case.

Finally, two days after Mark's arrest, the assistant state's attorney met with Mark and said, "Okay, Mr. Domechian, it's time for arraignment, and we have to get you to court. You will be charged with one count of using and conspiring to use a weapon of mass destruction. That is, namely, an improvised explosive device—or IED—against persons and property within the United States, resulting in death. I will also charge you with one count of malicious destruction of property by means of an explosive device, resulting in death. Once the charges are made, maybe we can work on a plea bargain. I also know that we have signed reports from two FBI agents that you saved their lives. So from then on, we can talk about what we can do, but I need names and dates and actions to make anything that you tell me worth negotiating."

"I will give you the name of the person who owned the business. Once you have him, we can talk about other conspirators in this plot," Mark said.

"I want names of foreign contacts as well," the assistant state's attorney said.

"When you are ready to deal, I will be ready to deal," Mark said.

"Give me the name, then," the assistant state's attorney said.

"Once we walk out of the arraignment, you will have it," Mark said.

The assistant state's attorney scowled and said, "Okay. We will be in court at 9:00 in the morning."

Chapter 57
The Scene

"I think by the end of the day today, we will have cleared the entire collapse area," the team leader of Illinois Task Force 1 said. "Once we have done that, we can extricate the rest of the bodies from the collapse area, and you can have the entire scene to process any other evidence that you want without my team getting in your way."

The Illinois Task Force 1 commander was Assistant Chief Darold Siemens from one of the fire departments in Chicago's western suburbs He and his men and women had been on the scene for the past three days. The work had been slow and painstaking partly because of the extent of the damage but also partly because all work had to be done with either an SCBA or an air-powered purifying respirator—or APR—because of the threat of radiation in the dust that they we constantly being exposed to. Illinois Task Force 1 was assigned the Richard J. Daley Center. The Boone County Fire Protection District from Missouri, the Los Angeles County Fire Department from California, and New York City teams were assisting Illinois Task Force 1.

Hazardous material teams from several MABAS divisions were operating near the two-square-block area acting mainly as decontamination teams for personnel and equipment leaving the scene.

IEMA's Radiological Response Task Force, The FBI's hazardous materials response team and teams from the United States Department of Energy and Argonne National Laboratory near Chicago were painstakingly combing the area, making extremely detailed maps of where the radiation had been located.

Laboratory analysis of the uranium used in the bomb indicated that it was an impure uranium from a Russian or Ukrainian enrichment facility. This fuel had been presumably lost or stolen when it was stored in a Ukrainian facility sometime during the fall of the Soviet Union. It was also determined that the fuel was not capable of fission because it had not been completely refined. It was, in fact, worthless as a fissionable source by United States standards, but it still had enough refinement that it could release radioactive products that were detectable. Mark had been scammed, but it did substantiate his claim about how he secured the materials.

The FBI was collecting evidence to determine how that bomb had been constructed and obtaining evidence for prosecution of the perpetrators.

Each worker and observer that left the area around the Richard J. Daley Center was carefully decontaminated. Most of the radioactive material was embedded in a straight-line path from the point of detonation. Nothing of the van was located, and no body parts from the occupant were ever found. The blast had literally disintegrated the van, the bomb, and Mr. B.

Trial and Commitment

Shannon Gentry, representatives from the mayor's staff, and representatives from Illinois emergency response agencies conducted regular news conferences from the OEMC media room. The room was large with various tiers in a semicircle around the speaker's podium. It resembled a tiered college classroom with a lot more technical capability. Satellite trucks from around the world had gathered in the media parking lot and three blocks from the scene around the James R. Thompson Center. Every major news organization did remote broadcasts from the city. Many national cable news programs did live broadcasts from the OEMC parking lot and from the area around the James R. Thompson Center. It was, in many ways, a media-driven frenzy to determine what exactly had happened.

The families of the victims had been located at McCormick Place. The deceased individuals were located at a temporary morgue established at the Chicago Department of Public Health. A disaster mortuary operational response team (DMORT) assembled at this location as well and worked out of the Chicago Department of Public Health offices. Autopsies and identification were conducted in Western Shelter tents in the parking lot of Chicago Department of Public Health. Team members from around the United States assembled as part of the DMORT activation. Many of the team members were seasoned veterans on many other tragic events. They all came together for one purpose, and that was to assist the FBI and identify victims for loved ones. The body of each deceased victim was autopsied, and the painstaking task of identification and retrieval of personal belongings was undertaken.

The media kept the morgue under constant scrutiny, hoping for any glimpse of a body being moved or a responder milling about so that they could question the individual. Staff were escorted by CPD into and out of the facility. A local food service company provided a refrigerated truck for storage of the human remains. The company name was left prominently on the side of the truck as the company that provided the truck offered it to the county as an in-kind gift. The trailers would never again be put in service.

The custom of burial was honored to the extent that it could be arranged. Many of the deceased left in private removal cars or coaches for transport to local funeral directors. The bodies were released as quickly as possible, but the Cook County Medical Examiner was the person whose signature made the transfer official for the body to be released to the family. The death toll was at 142, and close to one thousand patients had been or were being treated at hospitals throughout the Midwest. The farthest that patients had been transported was Springfield, Illinois, and those were patients being treated for burns.

The Richard J. Daley Center and all the buildings in a two-square-block area were closed, and the discussion of what to do with all the buildings in the area that had been initiated by the mayor's office. The mayor was lobbying Congress and the president to allow them to demolish the buildings and reconstruct the buildings in a manner to help beautify the area and provide for a memorial park area for the victims of the event.

A memorial service was held at McCormick Place a week after the event, where first responders and city and county government employees were honored. It was a packed house and was broadcast over all the major news channels. The president attended, as did officials from the city and state.

Michael and Marie watched from her hospital room.

Chapter 58
Apprehension

After his arraignment, Mark told the FBI about the operation that he had been part of. Simon and Nathan's identities and information were made available to Interpol and various law enforcement agencies throughout the United States.

Nathan's cell phone had been accessed, and since he had no idea that he would be apprehended or killed, no information had been deleted prior to the trip into the city. The phone proved to be a treasure trove of information.

The noose was tightening, and Agent Lattis had begged Special Agent Nettles to allow him to go when the call came in as to where Simon was located. Nettles and eventually Agent Krista Young agreed to allow Agent Lattis to travel and work on apprehending the mastermind. Lattis's arrest of Magomed had been reviewed, and the FBI director thought it best that the Chicago people initiate the arrest and custody of the suspect.

Simon's location had been determined from airport cameras in the United States and the UK. He was in London and was moving quickly to get to a foreign country where extradition would be impossible.

Agent Lattis received the call at two in the afternoon to be on a flight to London within the hour, and he was ready to go. His travel bags were packed.

Simon Waterson walked from the restroom to a seat located by the boarding gate. He looked at his ticket and at his watch.

Simon had been in London for three days, and it had been two since the bomb had been detonated. Simon had heard nothing from Nathan. What Simon had feared was surely true.

He reflected on his affiliation with Nathan and how they had become friends in the city of Montgomery, Alabama. Nathan had been so motivated by hatred when they had first met. He was a member of many pro-Aryan groups at that time. As their friendship grew, Nathan had become motivated to assist his friend Simon with the selling of arms. Simon viewed him as a true patriot. Nathan's hatred of the radical jihadists grew, and his distrust of the government grew as well.

How could this have happened to him? Simon thought. He fought off the intense feelings of loss that he was dealing with. Nathan had become like his younger brother. He knew that he would never see him again. Simon was sure that Mr. B. had been the triggerman, but he was also just as sure that Nathan had not been with him. Nathan was too smart for that, and he had so much to live for. This had not played out anything like what Simon had hoped for. He knew that he was alone and that it was time to go somewhere where his extradition to the United States would never be a possibility. He also thought of the business and his people. It was all behind him now. He had to focus. There was new direction!

A call came over the gate's message system. "We will be boarding Lufthansa flight 148 to Sharjah, United Arab Emirates, in just a few minutes. Please have your boarding passes ready."

Agent Lattis and Agent Macintyre were crossing the concourse when they saw him sitting quietly. The counterparts from the MI5 agency circled around to cross paths with Simon if needed.

Simon looked up. "May I help you?"

"I think you should come with me, Mr. Waterson," Agent Lattis said.

"And why would I do that?" Simon asked.

"As an agent of the Federal Bureau of Investigation and with cooperation from the British authorities, I have the right to retain you for questioning. The agents by the column over there will come over to assist me, and they are not quite as friendly as I am," Agent Lattis said.

Simon said nothing and turned to walk with Agents Lattis and Macintyre. The British agents walked behind as they left the boarding gate.

Simon sat in a small room with the agents asking him questions. He made no response. He looked quite content as he peered at the agents over his wire-rimmed glasses. His face was set like stone.

"I guess that is all we are going to get," one of the MI5 agents said.

Brian Lattis leaned over toward Simon and said, "Your bomb nearly killed my friend. He and I were in the car with your man Magomed."

Simon's eyes lit up. "Magomed is a traitor then!"

"He pulled us out of the car. He decided that murder was not on his list of crimes that he wanted to commit."

"Murder!" Simon stated. "Murder! How about justification for incompetence of the government and the fools that run it? Martyrdom for the cause of elimination of radicals with perverted ideals! Not murder!" Simon was livid.

Agent Lattis looked directly at Simon. "You are a fool!"

"I'll see you in hell, Lattis!" Simon stated. "You and all your so-called agents of freedom—or is it tyranny? You have no authority except that given to you by a corrupt government, under whose authority will you arrest me, Agent Lattis!"

Lattis looked intently at Simon for at least a minute. "I took an oath to defend the Constitution of the United States, and for that oath, I vowed to give my life if necessary. You took no oath, gave no vows except to engage in criminal activities that allowed you to line your own pockets with cash on the blood of innocents."

"You fools!" Simon yelled. "You had everything you needed to destroy the radicals and the jihadists. I—no, no, *we* gave you the perfect option. Nathan gave his life to help you get this job done, and you refused to use what we have given you to destroy the radicals that threaten the world. You could have tied the blast to the jihadists! It was in the palm of your hands, and you wasted it. You fools!"

Brian Lattis shook his head. "What a misconceived plan. You were wrong, and many people died because of you, including your friend Nathan. He died on the streets of Chicago, a testament to your betrayed friendship. He thought a lot of you. His cell phone showed how truly committed he was to you and your scheme. You betrayed him and all the others that died that day."

Simon put his head down. Agent Macintyre thought she heard a sob before she left the room.

Lattis walked out of the room.

According to a 2003 treaty between the United States and the UK, Simon was transported to the United States because of the overwhelming evidence presented in the United States District Court in Chicago.

Simon and Agent Lattis never spoke again throughout the flight or the movement into the jail and the courtrooms.

Simon was arraigned in the same courtroom that Mark was arraigned a few days before. His charges were the same as Mark's except that he was charged with over one hundred counts of murder, intent to commit murder, and use of a weapon of mass destruction to commit murder.

Attorney Lawrence Peterson was apprehended in Florida by FBI agents. He was sitting on a beach with a drink in his hand. He said nothing as he was arrested. He just smiled and walked toward the car. His friend the judge resigned the next day and was arrested as well.

Chapter 59
Sentencing

Magomed Domechian stood in front of the federal judge as he was to be sentenced.

"You have done some terrible things, and you have done some admirable things, and that is a great dilemma for this court to consider, Mr. Domechian," the judge said. "The federal prosecutor has dropped the charges dealing with using and conspiring to use a weapon of mass destruction against persons and property within the United States resulting in death. He also dropped the count of malicious destruction of property by means of an explosive device resulting in death, so he has levied lesser charges of money laundering and the intent to distribute material that may cause harm—mainly the fissionable material."

Mark was silent.

"However, your actions and statements will help to convict a man who was responsible for this heinous act, and I daresay that you yourself were a victim of this device. Also, your actions saved the lives of two federal employees, and I have signed testimony to that effect here in my hands." The judge held up two papers.

"So Mr. Domechian," the judge continued, "you can still go to jail for a very long time. Are you aware of this?"

Mark answered quietly, "Yes, ma'am, I am."

"There is one other letter that I have received on your behalf, and I questioned as to whether I should read it because I felt that the evidence was overwhelming, but I did read it. Do you know why I read it?" the judge asked.

"No, ma'am," answered Mark.

"Mr. Domechian, I read it because it was sent to me by a firefighter. A firefighter who, along with his team, gave my sister her life back a week ago on a busy Chicago interstate. She almost had her foot severed, and this firefighter and his team saved her life and that of her unborn child. I felt compelled to read it. This is what it said:

Dear Judge Gibson,

Mr. Domechian saved a life when there was no one else to do it. How I wished that I could have been there for Agent Lattis when their car was impacted by the blast wave, but I could not be there. Someone was, and he made a choice to act to save a life. When I went into the fire service, my family was not in favor of my career decision—all but one, that is, and his name is Agent Brian Lattis, but for twenty-two years, I have called him Uncle Brian. Magomed saved Uncle

Brian, and I feel that he deserves a chance to amend his life. Please consider my request for leniency for Mr. Domechian.

Signed,

Michael Fortenier

Mark looked back in the rear of the courtroom, and there was a young firefighter that Mark had seen twice before. He was sitting near Maggie with his dress uniform on, and he sat upright through the sentencing as though everything depended on the next few minutes. He was a committed young man that had played in part to Mark's decision to try to stop the plan. Michael smiled at Mark.

"I have considered all options," said the judge. "You can thank these two FBI agents and Mr. Fortenier that I don't throw the book at you right now. I will ask the officer of the court to see to it that you are handed over to the federal correctional system for a period not to exceed five years and credit time served with the Illinois Department of Corrections, and you will be eligible for parole in one year if your behavior indicates that you have earned such privileges." The gavel hit the desk, and the proceedings were over.

Mark was silent.

Maggie was sobbing in the back of the room.

Agent Brian Lattis was silent.

Mark turned to Lattis and said, "You have given me a chance that I will not take lightly."

Lattis looked at Mark. "You gave me my life. It isn't a fair trade."

"I thought life wasn't fair. I abused the chances I was given. Good people make life fair, and they make it worth living," Mark replied.

Maggie had walked to the front of the courtroom to be with Mark and Brian Lattis. Lattis handed Mark a picture of two young people standing by a garden gate.

Mark looked at the photo with tears in his eyes. He showed the picture to Maggie. "My sister Aysa," Mark said.

"She is living with a soldier in the southern part of Russia," Lattis said. "I talked to Duncan's friend in the Foreign Intelligence Service, and he gave me this picture. By his account, they are happy, and he will be an officer soon. So she has a good life, but she thinks you and your father are dead." He looked at Mark. "Maggie and I haven't forgotten about our other deal, and we will work on that soon."

"Thank you," Mark said, "and please let him know that I am not living with the pigs anymore."

Brian Lattis smiled. Maggie hugged Mark, and the law enforcement officers began to walk him out of the room.

Agent Lattis walked to the back of the courtroom and greeted Michael. "Thanks for writing the letter, Michael."

Trial and Commitment

Mark stopped and shook Michael's hand as well. "I can't believe what you did for me. Why did you do it?"

"I felt that you have a good heart, and Uncle Brian is alive because of you," Michael said.

Mark looked at Michael. "I thought of your courage and commitment, and that was part of the reason I tried to stop the bombing. I'm sorry I failed."

"Failure is a relative thing. That's what Uncle Brian told me when I was young," Michael said. "Best of luck to you."

"Thank you," Mark said as he was escorted away. Maggie smiled at Michael.

"You can spend some time with him each week if you want to," Lattis said.

"I know," Maggie said through the tears. "I will wait for him. I promised him that."

"I'm sure that you will," Lattis said.

"You don't have to go with me, Brian. I can do this myself," Maggie said.

"I wouldn't miss it for the world," Lattis said. "I'll pick you up on Saturday."

Chapter 60
Release from the Hospital

Agent Duncan Furgeson was taken to the hospital entrance by his daughter and a nurse. He was in a wheelchair but was able to walk through the door. He had suffered some setbacks, including a mild stroke that had left part of his left side partially paralyzed.

There were several agents there to greet him, and Agent Brian Lattis and Special Agent Nettles were in front of the rest.

"It's a good day," Duncan Furgeson said to the other agents. "A good day to go home."

Duncan had been briefed on all the events that had happened with Mark and the others that had been arrested. His only comment was, "I should have been in court that day as well."

Brian Lattis said, "It wasn't like you could have just gotten up and gone. The nurses would have tackled you at the door."

They both laughed.

"Really, Duncan," Lattis said, "the statements carried the most weight, and it's not like you can't go see him when you get stronger."

Special Agent Nettles helped get Furgeson to his car. "You take as long as you need, Duncan; we can carry on without you for a while."

"You will want me back soon, sir, to help keep Brian out of trouble." Duncan had not lost his sense of humor.

Lattis laughed and smacked his boss on the back. Special Agent Nettles gave Lattis a quick smile and a stern look. Agent Brian Lattis knew life was back to some stage of normal.

Duncan got in the car with his daughter, and they drove to his apartment on the South Side of Chicago. His law enforcement days were far from over.

Marie and Michael were going to the front entrance of Rush University Medical Center. Marie's leg was still in a brace, but all the tubes had been removed, and the leg itself was half the size of what it had been with the infection that had developed after the metal was removed. Marie had no fever, and she was feeling well and had asked to go home for the past few days.

She had had a steady stream of visitors, including people from the television station. The news had not been good. Eight people from the station had died in the event, including the two individuals that Michael had discovered in the studio. There were others hospitalized with various injuries, but most of them had been released from the hospital. The other news stations in Chicago had donated equipment to help the station reconstitute itself in a rented studio near the James R. Thompson Center.

Marie had been offered a spot on the anchor desk until she was well enough to begin traveling around the city again. Marie accepted with the condition that Sydney be assigned to her as a researcher and writer, and the management had agreed.

As they made their way to the lobby, Marie hugged the nurses that had been with her from the beginning. "Good luck, Marie," they all said.

As Michael and Marie got closer to the entrance, Marie looked up at Michael, who was pushing the wheelchair, and asked, "What's this?"

Three engine companies had assembled at the door of the lobby in the parking area. As the two of them made their way out of the hospital, the firefighters began to clap and cheer.

Marie was shocked. "Michael! Oh my!"

Marie was greeted by some of the people that had been with her since the rescue. Many of them had been repeat visitors to the hospital.

Cassie was the first to hug her. "Good luck, Marie!" Cassie had been there many days and had relieved Michael when he needed some rest. In the process, Cassie and Marie had become great friends.

Cliff and DJ were there, as was Captain Smith, who hugged Marie and said, "You are a great lady, Marie!"

Julie and David were there as well. Marie hugged each of them.

Sydney was there, and as she hugged Marie, she began to cry. "I knew we could do it. I told you Michael would come!"

Tom Gibson had made the trip from Springfield just to be there. "Cliff told me that you were going home, and I just had to come," Tom said. He and Cliff had become good friends.

Marie's parents were there, as were Michael's parents. They hugged Marie, and everyone was smiling.

As they got into Marie's car for the trip to her apartment, Michael looked at Captain Smith. "Once I get her home and settled in, I will be back to the station."

Captain Smith told Michael, "Don't worry about that; we have someone who put in to cover the shift." He looked at David and smiled.

"I have his culinary needs taken care of as well." David smiled. "A salad and some nice fresh pasta!" He laughed.

Captain Smith laughed with the firefighters. "We'll see about that!" he said.

Marie and Michael went to Marie's apartment, and Michael helped Marie get everything situated. She was tired, so they sat and watched television and enjoyed the view of Lake Michigan.

Chapter 61
Ekazhevo

In the village of Ekazhevo, Brian Lattis and Maggie were led to a small farmhouse.

The Russian agent knocked on the door, and a small voice said, "Come in."

"You have guests from America, sir," the Russian agent said.

The old gentleman looked up at Brian Lattis and Maggie. "I don't know you."

"We are friends of your son," Maggie said.

The old man looked intently at them. "I don't know where he is."

"We do," Lattis said. "Aysa as well."

The old man's eyes lit up. "You are from the American police?"

"I am an FBI agent," Lattis said.

The old man said, "I will listen to what you have to say."

They sat and talked with him for over an hour. Mark showed him a picture of Aysa and gave him a letter that Mark had sent for him. It said simply, "I have finally listened to your holy man, and I have come home."

"Will you come with us?" Maggie asked.

The old man looked at the floor for a long time. "You have come all this way to tell me about my son and Aysa. I am grateful to you, but this is where I live, and I can now live the rest of my days in peace knowing that my children are at peace. Tell my son that I never doubted that one day he would come home, and now I know he has."

They visited with him for a while longer and went their way. Brian Lattis laid an envelope on the table that he and Duncan Furgeson had put together. It was enough American dollars to keep the Mark's father fed and clothed for quite a while, at least until Mark was released from prison.

Mark was glad to hear that at last his father was at peace with him and with the world.

Chapter 62
A Life Together

Michael hurried home after his abbreviated shift. He cleaned up and hurried to pick up Marie.

"What's the rush, Michael?" Marie asked.

"I told you, honey … dinner," Michael said.

They drove to the restaurant.

"It's crowded in here tonight," Marie said. "Look at all these cars! Wait a minute, I know these cars. These are our friends."

"C'mon," Michael said. "I have reservations."

"So do I!" said Marie.

"It's okay. C'mon." Michael gently kissed her on the cheek.

As they walked into the restaurant, everyone stood up and cheered.

"What is going on here?" Marie asked Michael.

Captain Smith and his wife, Tammy; David and Julie; Cliff and his fiancée, Jennie; DJ and his wife, Alea; Cassie; and Freddie and his friend Alana, whom Michael had met at the fire academy on training day, were all there. Marie also saw Sydney and one of the station crew and both sets of parents, and even Uncle Brian Lattis and his wife, Emily, were there. They were all sitting around two tables. They all cried out, "Happy birthday!"

Marie looked at Michael with a look of disbelief. "Honey, it's not my birthday."

"What?" Michael said. "I thought … oh no."

Marie was really perplexed as suddenly Michael dropped to one knee. "Well, I guess since it isn't your birthday, then I guess we'd better make the most of it." He pulled out a small box from his pocket and opened it to reveal a small but very brilliant diamond.

"I think that *Marie Fortenier* would have a nice ring to it," he said. "Please, Marie, please be my wife?"

Marie was in awe. She hugged Michael and said, "Yes!"

The crowd erupted in applause and laughter.

Their adventure was just beginning.

Acknowledgement

Thanks to everyone who helped me complete this book especially to:

Kerry P who inspired the character "Cassie". You're the best.

To the personnel of the Chicago Fire Department
who let me be part of your training team

To my sons Christian and Connor who helped
me to realize what life is really about.

To my friend Connor whose enthusiasm was
a real motivation to do my best

To Gary who helped me with the radiological component of the text

To Jane who encouraged me to write on

To Ben, Drew, Madi and Matt for your
encouragement and proofreading

To Allison who read the text and helped me
edit it. You will be a great editor!

To my sister who helped me get this project off the ground

To all the firefighters, EMS personnel and law enforcement
personnel that I have worked with, taught and above
all, learned from. This is your book as well.

Printed in the United States
By Bookmasters